ARE YOU NOW
OR HAVE YOU
EVER BEEN?

ADVANCE PRAISE

"*Are You Now, or Have You Ever Been?* perfectly highlights the rare talent of Farkas. A modern-day Vonnegut, Farkas is able to put forth giant philosophical questions in ways that are heightened by his intellect and humor while still being accessible to those of us without our PhDs. It is rare to find a smart person, rarer still to find a smart person who is funny, and it is almost impossible to find a smart person who is funny and able to connect to a common person without sacrificing his wit. This collection is a treasure of hilarious, existential terror and longing."

—Jesi Bender, author of *Kinderkrankenhaus*
and *The Book of the Last Word*

"The fictions in Andrew Farkas' *Are You Now, or Have You Ever Been?* may upon some slight reflection seem to invite comparisons to Coover, Borges, at times, Beckett—the multivalent ingenuity and impressive command of voice in these fictions are immediately obvious—but such comparisons can't fully capture the sheer generosity of this brilliantly disorienting, funny, and ultimately sui generis investigation into identity. If you somehow haven't ever been a fan of Farkas before, you are now."

—Gabriel Blackwell, author of
Doom Town and *Correction*

"Absurd and quizzical, Farkas' stories play with what stories are and can be, but paradoxically by the very act of doing so unearth something endearingly (and flawedly, if flawedly is a word—spoiler: it's not) human."

—Brian Evenson, author of *The Glassy, Burning Floor
of Hell* and *Song for the Unraveling of the World*

"I'm not the kind of person who smugly delights in the suffering of others, but Andrew Farkas' collected characters rock a capacious, capricious, ambulatory despair, whispered telephonically from beneath an indescribable Midwestern sky out to the very edge of the expanded universe. Each story's iteration has its own unexpected punchline: a warehouse is a bar is stamped and certified dead. And when tomorrow finally arrives—late, as usual, and frumpy and still involuntarily single—the apocalypse knock knocks, and although the sky might be dreadfully common, these stories are majestic."

—Lily Hoàng, author of *Underneath* and *A Bestiary*

"Andrew Farkas is an infernal calculating engine producing in *Are You Now, or Have You Ever Been?* a mess o' finely machined machine-like fictions. There is a sublime relentlessness in the generative power of the permutations at all levels from word to sentence to paragraph to page. He exhausts exhaustion effortlessly. These inventive hypoxic hieroglyphs gin-up ingeniously a whole new notion of the genus: story and the species: short."

—Michael Martone, author of *Plain Air: Sketches from Winesburg, Indiana* and editor of *The Complete Writings of Art Smith, the Bird Boy of Fort Wayne*

"Albert Camus' *The Stranger* meets George Saunders' *Tenth of December*: *Are You Now, or Have You Ever Been?* gifts the reader with the playful humor of a head-scratcher without a head. Baffling, absurdist, philosophical, existential, and hilariously disturbing, in this collection, the paradox of finding the self morphs 'the other,' daring to ask how we reach the core of identity when our center keeps shifting."

—Aimee Parkison, author of *Suburban Death Project* and *Sister Séance*

"Farkas' serial subjectivities inspect the rigid core of the rubbery stuff we call consciousness. This is a funny, playful, ultimately quite serious book about the places and ways we meet, as well as the time that swipes everything back."

—Hugh Sheehy, author of *Design Flaw* and *The Invisibles*

ARE YOU NOW OR HAVE YOU EVER BEEN?

Stories

ANDREW FARKAS

Alternating Current Press
Boulder, Colorado

Copyright © 2026 Alternating Current Press
Copyright © 2026 Andrew Farkas
All rights reserved

Published by Alternating Current Press
Boulder, Colorado 80302
altcurrentpress.com
All rights reserved

ISBN-13 (paperback): 978-1-946580-57-3
ISBN-10 (paperback): 1-946580-57-0
ISBN-13 (hardcover): 978-1-946580-58-0
ISBN-13 (ebook): 978-1-946580-59-7

Cover artwork: Patter Hill and Leah Angstman © 2026
Author photo: Nick Krug © 2024, 2026

The following is a work of fiction created by the author. All names, individuals, places, items, brands, events, characters, etc., are the product of the author's imagination, are used fictiously, or are entirely coincidental.

No part of this publication may be reproduced, stored in a retrieval system, or transmitted, in any form or by any means, electronic, mechanical, photocopied, recorded, or otherwise, without the prior permission of Alternating Current Press, except for the quotation of brief passages used inside of an article, criticism, or review.

Printed in the United States of America

10 9 8 7 6 5 4 3 2 1

TABLE OF CONTENTS

Preface 13

Way Out 19
Timbuktu 20
Delusions of Nandeur 26
Bastille Day 38
Life Insurance 40
An Immaterial Message 54
The Committee for
    Standing on Shoulders 57
The Divine Plan: Notes for an
    Unperformable Mise-en-Scène 68
A Sky Party 77
Astray 86
A Name You Can Trust 89
Identity Theft 125
Oubliette 129
To Build a Fire ... in Space 146
The First Circumnavigator 151
A Rogue Department
    Course Offering 162
Is This the Ship of Theseus? 166
Written with You
    Sitting Next to Me 176
The Last Light You'll See 179

for someone or other, certainly

That's why I'm sitting here with you—because you remind me of you. Your eyes, your throat, your lips! Everything about you reminds me of you. Except you. How do you account for that?

—Groucho Marx,
A Night at the Opera (1935)

PREFACE

In 2008, when I began my PhD at the University of Illinois at Chicago, I had written two collections of short fiction: *Sunsphere* and *Self-Titled Debut*. I honestly thought they'd be published in that respective order, giving me the chance to say in a bio, *"Self-Titled Debut* is Andrew Farkas' second book." The joke was on me, though, because after walking in the rain across my new campus, I ducked into a computer lab (my Nokia certainly couldn't check email) and learned, from Professor Elisabeth Sheffield, that my manuscript had won the Subito Press contest. Which meant that *Self-Titled Debut* was to be my first book.

Subito Press was operated by the University of Colorado at Boulder's graduate creative-writing program, and the experience of working with Elisabeth and the student editors was wonderful. Later, while in Boulder giving a reading after the book was released, I stayed at the Hotel Boulderado (the perfect place to stage a whodunit, which I, alas, missed by one day), drank in a bar that looked like catacombs, and ate fish-and-chips made of salmon. I wouldn't publish another book for ten years: my novel, *The Big Red Herring*, and, at last!, *Sunsphere*.

Near the end of the Covid-19 pandemic lockdown, I sadly learned that Subito Press was going on an indefinite hiatus, making me wonder if my *Self-Titled Debut* would fade into obscurity. Luckily, at the 2021 Kansas Book Festival, I met Leah Angstman, who told me her press considered reprints. And so, Alternating Current Press jolted new life into my first collection, for which I am eternally grateful. The original collection contained the following pieces: "An Immaterial Message," "Delusions of Nandeur," "Life Insurance," "The Committee for Standing on

Shoulders," "The Divine Plan," "A Name You Can Trust," "Oubliette," "To Build a Fire ... in Space," "Timbuktu," and "The Last Light You'll See."

For the reprint, Leah and I decided to include more of my stories, the ones that weren't in *Sunsphere* and that don't jibe with the book I'm currently writing (a collection focused on cinematic tropes called *Movies Are Fine for a Bright Boy like You*). The newly added stories are: "Way Out," "Bastille Day," "A Sky Party," "Astray," "Identity Theft," "The First Circumnavigator," "A Rogue Department Course Offering," "Is This the Ship of Theseus?," and "Written with You Sitting Next to Me." Plus, seeing as how this book is no longer my debut, we decided on a new title: *Are You Now, or Have You Ever Been?*

The titles of both collections connect to the fact that all of these stories are, in some way, about identity, about the difficulty of defining the self, about how we often mistake ourselves for someone else, about the hazards of defining the self too clearly. In a world that gets more obsessed with identity every day, I hope these stories decenter our understanding, I hope they show just how difficult it truly is to know ourselves, I hope they help people accept that the search for a self is a lifetime quest.

I experienced this not-so-much identity crisis, but more like identity confusion, upon editing the works from my first book. Reading through, I found myself wanting to talk to the author, to ask why he'd made the decisions he'd made, to critique his sensibilities (for he's nowhere near as sophisticated as I am now), to hear finally a clear explanation as to why he chose to publish under "Andrew" Farkas, seeing as how I've *always* gone by Andy (I even have my students call me Andy). But when I reached out to him, I found Andrew Farkas was unavailable. Or, perhaps, he just hasn't checked back in to the computer lab yet.

And so, whereas I have edited those early works, I have done so lightly. I wouldn't want to receive a monstrously long email explaining how I'd screwed everything up from none other than Andrew Farkas.

Whoever he might be.

Lawrence, Kansas
2023

ARE YOU NOW OR HAVE YOU EVER BEEN?

WAY OUT

At one point during the tour, They showed me the door.

"This is the way you get out," They told me.

"But I am not here," I said.

They thought about this. It was true.

"It could also be the way you get in," They said.

"Is this the way in, then?" I asked.

"No," They said. "It is the way you get out."

TIMBUKTU

Go to Timbuktu—an island paradise.
Stand on the beach. Gaze at the beauty of the sun shining upon the crystal-blue water, the white sand. It will blind you. But gaze upon it. You'll be glad you did. While you're blind, reaching for sunglasses, hat, greenshade visor (are you a greenshade visor kind of person?, wonder), think about the Walrus and the Carpenter's plan to clean up the beach; think about how an hourglass company would clean up here. Here, do not think about the past; do not worry about the future. Instead, think only of the present. Of the brilliant shining sun. Of the opalescent waves. Of the bleached, rolling dunes in the distance. Let yourself fade away.

Enjoy the weather of Timbuktu.
    Walk across the island. Notice how the temperature is exactly what you'd want it to be if someone asked you. Do not think about how no one ever asks

you—about anything. How most things occur against your will. Instead, realize that throughout Timbuktu, the temperature varies from 64° to 95°. Depending on your taste, you can experience any climate at any time. There is even snow on top of Mount Timbuktu, and the dunes of the beach wrap around and form a small desert. But for most it is perpetually spring and summer, and summer and spring. Do not think about how your own seasons are winter and fall without end, how the days are getting shorter and shorter year-round. Instead, bask in the constant light, in the climate that almost seems designed for you and you alone.

Plan a family gathering in Timbuktu.

Near where the beach meets the boardwalk, see a wedding party. The bride dressed in white, the groom in black. Wonder if there has ever been a wedding where the bride wore black, the groom white. Think of a marriage ceremony where both wear gray. (Do not think about your own relationships.) Weddings are joyous events the world over, but especially in Timbuktu. Here, family and friends come together in paradise to celebrate a union that will never be broken. Do not think about the fifty-percent divorce rate. Do not think about your own failing (failed) marriage. Do not think about how your spouse cheated on you for years. Do not think about the bitter divorce proceedings. Instead, watch the end of the ceremony. Catch the bouquet. Do not think about pollen allergies. Instead, hand the bouquet to a cute little girl. Hug the bride. Shake the groom's hand. Welcome them to Timbuktu as if you owned the place. Leave the happy couple with a quiet tip of your greenshade visor.

Timbuktu has gourmet restaurants and classy lounges.

Stop off at one of our local watering holes. Enjoy an aperitif. Wonder if the predinner drink has such a fancy name so people can sound sophisticated while consuming alcohol on an empty stomach. Have a large meal (or a light snack) prepared by our culinary experts at one of our fine eateries. Do not think about how many people are starving in the world. Do not think about why it's still necessary to get drunk when you're away from your dark, depressing home life. Instead, indulge in a decadent piece of chocolate cake. You'll be glad you did. Go to a bar. Have a rum drink. Hit on a member of the opposite sex. On a member of the same sex. Do not drink straight rum by yourself. Do not drink out of the bottle. Wonder how you got back to your hotel room. Wonder who put the green-shade visor on you.

Play nine or eighteen on our world-famous golf links.

Relax your legs. Take an athletic stance. Grip the club firmly but not too tight. Plant your feet. Keep your arms straight. Bring your arms back. Keep your eye on the ball. Bring your weight back. Keep your eye on the ball. Bring your arms forward. (Keep your eye on the ball.) Bring your weight forward. Keep your arms straight. Follow through. Sand trap. Do not think about the hourglasses. Do not think about the minutes of your life that are draining away. Do not think about how you could use your time more wisely. Do not think about the little oysters, tricked by the promise of fun into following the Walrus and the Carpenter to certain doom. Pick up the club. You can get out of the sand trap. Give yourself more credit. You'll be glad you did. Water hazard. Do not think "repeat ad nauseam."

Try your luck at Timbuktu's glamorous casino.

Do not think about how your luck has been so rotten lately. Do not think about how money doesn't buy happiness—for that's a cliché. Do not think about the look of quiet desperation on everyone's face. Do not think about the cacophonous sound generated by the slot machines. And how that sound is a siren for suckers (the poor oysters). Do not think about the lives of the natives, or of those who cannot afford a paradise-island getaway. Do not sit down at a table, any table, with a stack of one-hundred-dollar bills and throw them out there until they're gone as if your losses were preordained. Instead, pursue lady luck. Believe in lady luck. Have fun. You'll be glad you did.

There is always something to do in Timbuktu.

Walk around the island in the late afternoon. See people fishing. Windsurfing. Parasailing. Swimming. Sunbathing. Playing tennis. Playing volleyball. Eating. Drinking. Do not think about how you never fit in anywhere. How everything you try becomes a failure, seems doomed to fail from the beginning. Instead, witness the beautiful sunset while sitting in a watering hole covered with aged maps. Do not wonder about your place in the world.

The perfect location—Timbuktu.

Timbuktu is not on the equator, although located at 0° latitude. Timbuktu is between the tropics, but it is not close to the tropics—it is far enough away to be considered outside the tropics. Timbuktu is near none of the continents, except for three of them. Timbuktu's tropical climate is due to a particular jet stream that cuts through the north and the south, while being an eastern westerly. Timbuktu is a lone island in an archipelago. Timbuktu is closer than you think.

Join us in Timbuktu for the celebration of Festival.

Festival is the festival of celebrations. It is said, on this day, many years ago, before Timbuktu was "discovered" by Ponce de León during his quest for the elusive Fountain of Youth, even before the original discovery of Timbuktu by the Viking Leif de León (an ancestor of Ponce), the people celebrated the first Festival. And so, Festival was born in commemoration of this day. Drink a rum drink in honor of this traditional celebration. Walk around the luau. See the children playing with the traditional Festival dolls. Do not think about your lost childhood. Do not think about your children leading lost lives. Do not think.

Visit the mysterious mountain café of Timbuktu.

Leave the festival of Festival. Gaze upon Mount Timbuktu. Climb to the top. Do not spill your drink. Throw away your greenshade visor. It doesn't suit you. At the top, find a natural café playfully called The Cabbage King. The café was carved out of the rock of the mountain by erosion. The sheet metal, the glass windows, the slippery-shiny red stools, the large booths, even the neon sign are all part of the mountain itself. Absolutely authentic. Even the soda fountain. Even the soda jerk. Formed by wind and water erosion. Gaze upon this from the darkness. Do not think about death. Do not think about death. Do not think about death. Do not think about death. Instead, order their specialty: the vanilla milkshake with Hershey's chocolate syrup

—all naturally occurring from the erosion of the mountain. (Do not think about death. Do not think about death.) Walk in through the naturally occurring glass and metal doors and sit on a naturally occurring vinyl stool. (Do not think about death. Do not think about death.) Look the soda jerk in the eye. Remember that knowing people always gets you something. Tell him Roy sent ya.

Go to Timbuktu—an island paradise.

Because of the beauty of Timbuktu, because of how hospitable the natives are, many of our visitors have been to Timbuktu before, have returned to relive their vacations in paradise, to visit their old friends, to meet new. So many of our visitors are repeat visitors, perhaps you have been to Timbuktu before, perhaps you have made friends, perhaps you have only forgotten, perhaps your friends, both visitors and natives alike, surrounded by oyster shells from their hors d'oeuvres, are waiting for you at your favorite watering hole, ironically wearing greenshade visors, hoisting a traditional Festival rum aperitif in your honor. Perhaps. Go to Timbuktu. Find out. You'll be glad you did.

DELUSIONS OF NANDEUR

> Insane asylums are filled with people who think they're Jesus or Satan. Very few have delusions of being a guy down the block who works for an insurance company.
> —*Confessions of a Dangerous Mind* (2002)

THE HOLE AT THE RESIDENCE ON THE CUL-DE-SAC ILE, 27 FEBRUARY, 1815

Out the window, he sees men digging. He stands with his arms behind his back, his left wrist in his right hand. The earth removed from the hole is thick clay, chunks of which are stacked nearby rather than in the usual uniform pile of soil. The hole is rectangular; the stack of chunks is formless. But the rain beats down, so the clay may yet fuse into a whole.

The man at the window says:

"For all intents and purposes, Monsieur Vizir, I now know I am *not* an insurance salesman named 'Bernard Nandeur.' But from April 1814 to the present, I certainly thought I was. In a way, I still do, although I have been given ample evidence to the contrary. So, whereas I do not *feel* it, I am convinced this is a case of mistaken identity: I am mistaken about my own identity. But who are we really? Are we who we think we are, or who we are proven to be? I do not know. ..."

He continues watching the men out the window. The rain stops.

A Meeting with Jean-Baptiste Bessières on Le Voie du Sphynx, 1 April, 1814

"Monsieur Bessières, whatever happened to this statue?"

"The nose, sir, it was shot off."

"By whom, Monsieur Bessières?"

"Wasn't it by you, sir, when you were young?"

"For one, please call me Bernard, not 'sir.'"

"Bernard?"

"For two, I believe we can agree that history is a set of lies agreed upon?"

"Indeed."

"And in these days, the invention of printing and the diffusion of knowledge render historical calumnies a little less dangerous?"

"I believe so, sir."

"Bernard."

"As you wish."

"Truth will always prevail in the long run, I do believe."

"As do I."

"But how slow its progress!"

"Alas."

"Yet, that is what the Organization is for. That is why you, my good friend, need insurance."

"Insurance, sir? I mean: Insurance, Bernard?"

"Thank you. Yes, insurance. It seeks the Truth, it finds the Truth, it ensures the Truth. And when no one else knows what the Truth is, the Organization assembles the clues and creates the Truth."

"I say."

"Do not be lost amidst the lies. I did not shoot the nose off that statue."

"I see."

"Now, allow me to expound upon some policies that are in your utmost interest."

"My interest ... Bernard?"

"Absolutely, the interest of the Truth."

"The truth ..."

AN EXPLANATION TO M. CYRUS OF THE BOULEVARD TOULON, 3 MAY, 1814

"With the Organization, Monsieur Cyrus, you needn't worry that your beliefs or your thoughts will counter our own. No one should be afraid to be exactly who they are. The Organization believes in freedom. Nothing is more difficult, and therefore more precious, than to be able to decide. So, Monsieur Cyrus, unlike other more tyrannical firms (the Bourbon Insurance Agency, for instance), the Organization leaves you free to do whatever you wish, as long as you do not harm anyone in the process. Now when I say 'anyone,' however, I include yourself in that statement. You are not free to hurt yourself. The Organization's policies aim to protect all life. Certainly, you agree with us on this point. Who wouldn't agree? So, not only will we cover you should an unfortunate accident occur, but also, we will encourage you to take care of yourself (something which, we know, you aim to do, anyhow). Our encouragement comes in monetary form; if you let yourself go, we shall raise your premiums; if you ... do yourself in, we will negate your policies, leaving your family destitute. The conscience is the inviolable asylum of the liberty of man, Monsieur Cyrus. Thus, I am certain you understand that, as long as you are bringing no harm to yourself or anyone else, as long as you heed your conscience, then you are perfectly free to do and think as you wish."

The Drawers at the Residence on Cul-de-Sac Ile, 25 February, 1815

They are all open in a manner that suggests steps.

    A man sleeps in a four-poster bed nearby. It is dark. There is the sound of water in the distance. The moon shines through the windows. With a start, he wakes, rubs his eyes, swings his short legs over the side of the bed, looks at the drawers, frowns. Up from the bed, he walks to the drawers, places a hand on the topmost (and least opened) drawer, glances inside: a blue waistcoat.

He frowns deeper. The moon shines through the windows. More and more and more clothing litters the floor as he removes each piece with increasing rapidity. Something is lost. Or someone must have replaced his clothes with someone else's. Or perhaps he is lost, in the wrong room. For, based on the confusion and concern displayed, the man made by these clothes is not the man going through them. He looks about the room, spinning wildly, with each turn finding he is still in the same place. Now, he stuffs the clothes back into the drawers. He peers around, creeping along, looking for something, but only finds that the drawers are open. He closes all but one of them, which remains slightly ajar. In bed, he cannot rest, tossing and turning. He gets up, stumbles against the drawers, closing the last one. In seconds he is asleep. The moon shines through the windows. There is a sound of water in the distance.

A Meeting with Jean Lannes on the Amiens Impasse, 14 June, 1814

"Who I am, Monsieur Lannes, is of little importance."
"What?"
"It is true, I am your insurance agent."
"Insurance agent?"
"Yes, that is all. My name is of little importance."
"I beg to differ."
"Please, Monsieur Lannes, you flatter me. And he who knows how to flatter also knows how to slander."
"I do say, I would never slander you, sir."
"Even if you did, it would matter little."
"Why?"

"Because it is the Organization that matters. When I am gone, the Organization will remain. Ideas are of the greatest importance. They *should* outlast, outrank those who conceive of them. The Idea, the Organization, will forever be the star of the people's rights, the voice of their efforts, the motto of their hopes. It has attained the Glory only an Idea can attain, and my mission is to further that Glory—although obscurity is forever ... and I am obscure."

"I think I get you, sir. I ..."

"I am more a meteorite than a comet."

"... I ... I do say ..."

"If I hadn't been born Bernard Nandeur, I could have been anyone else."

"A good one, sir; what about ...?"

"Isn't it a beautiful day?"

"... Beautiful day? Oh. Oh, yes, it is."

"I am glad you are willing to live in the present."

"Why is that, sir?"

"For the stupid speak of the past, fools speak of the future, but only the wise speak of the present. And you have made a wise decision today, a decision that firmly plants you in the present. I thank you for buying ..."

"I haven't purchased anything."

"Please, don't think of it that way. You have used your wisdom to buy peace of mind."

An Explanation to M. Artaxerxes of Rue de l'Ulcère Espagnol, 14 July, 1814

"Few things are brought to a successful issue by impetuous desire, Monsieur Artaxerxes, but most by calm and prudent forethought. That forethought, in my case, is the insurance policy. Think of it, sir. The sovereignty of the people is inalienable. Yet they need a guide to assist them. And what better guide than that which they select themselves? The problem with the Bourbons was that they lacked the Organization's approach. We do not go to the people; they come to us. And one day, when the government requires our services, the people will not blame us; they will blame the government. Or, even better, they will blame someone or something else. After all, monsieur, as you know, we are here to help you. That is our business. People come to insurance companies, particularly the Organization, for peace of mind; they want to feel safe. Our policies may be short, yet obscure, but that is because people do not care for long explanations; long explanations bore and confuse them. Brevity, apparent security—that is what men want. Furthermore, and I say this to you in the strictest confidence as you are one of my best clients: Men, in general, are but children of a larger growth. Now, although there are children who learn quite well via intellectual means, there are those who must be coerced. So, not only do people seek us out, but also, they are made better by finding us, by following our policies. You can have your morality, your law enforcement, your religion. Insurance, that is what makes men stay honest."

A LESSON WITH M. TALMA ON THE CUL-DE-SAC ILE, 27 FEBRUARY, 1815

A Public Comportment Coach, Monsieur Talma's moves are smooth and graceful, yet masculine. Everything about them is measured, and if they are not practiced, if they are not mastered, they require such cogitation as to be impossible. Keep the legs straight but not too straight. Know where your hands are and why they are there. Keep your eyes fixed forward but cast slightly upward so as to appear thoughtful. Keep a grave look upon your face, but occasionally allow a spot of mirth to appear—that way people won't think you an automaton. Walk neither quickly nor slowly, so no one will know whether you are on an important mission or merely sauntering to the lavatory. Small, personal gestures should be crisp, quick, and purposeful. Grand gestures should be gradual, broad, and puissant. Always remember the strictures of Aeschines. Never appear lost, even if you are, hopelessly.

When the movements, postures, and poses of M. Talma are followed, they can transform a man of 5'6" into a Roman senator.

A Meeting with Édouard Mortier on Aspern-Essling Avenue, 22 September, 1814

"Monsieur Mortier, I have decided not to accept my promotion."

"Promotion? What the devil …"

"It is too kind of you, sir."

"What are you …"

"I know you are flabbergasted, sir. But I feel I am not yet ready. And since the torment of precautions often exceeds the dangers to be avoided, I believe it is best to abandon myself to destiny instead of abusing your good graces. Monsieur Alexander and Monsieur Auguste, they are much more adept than I am."

"Who?"

"Furthermore, I am a man of the people."

"A man of the … Certainly, a man of the people."

"And an agent should sacrifice the best affections of his heart for the good of the Organization."

"I think I get you. …"

"No sacrifice should be above his determination."

"Indeed."

"Such an agent brings esteem to a firm, for public esteem is the recompense of an honest firm."

"What are we talking about, sir?!"

"I feel my place is outside of the office, not as a manager behind a desk."

"Are you completely mad?!"

"I am completely even-tempered."

An Explanation to M. Cid of Le Roi de Rome Corridor, 1 November, 1814

"Nothing renders an agency so despicable as religious despotism, Monsieur Cid. It is worse than the tactics of the Bourbon firm, for it even more neglects the interests and rights of the people. But I believe God has given us the will to overcome all obstacles. And when I say 'us,' I mean the Organization. For we are like a secular religion. We reward the good and the meek; we punish the bad and the aggressive. We encourage acts of benevolence. We advocate honesty, purity, fidelity, sobriety. We discourage mendacity, corruption, incontinence, vice. Monsieur Cid, we promise recompense to those who obey our strictures but who encounter misfortune; we promise damnation to those who violate our laws. We define the world in a way that comforts our customers, confuses our competitors, and enrages our enemies. We impose form where before the masses saw only chaos. Through the services delineated in our policies, the Organization conjoins its clients (the true believers) into one whole."

A Meeting with Michel Ney on Austerlitz Ruelle, 26 February, 1815

"There is a revolution afoot!"
 "A revolution?"
 "A revolution!"
 "Vive la révolution!"
 "And it is called 'Absolute Insurance.'"
 "Absolute insurance?"
 "Absolute Insurance, Monsieur Ney. For, as you know, insurance protects, but Absolute Insurance protects absolutely."
 "I believe we must talk."

An Explanation to M. Vizir on Le Place Marengo, 15 March, 1815

The sun shines down on the solid square, constructed of one vast piece of stone, cracked over time by the scores and scores of citizens who've traversed it. Flags of blue, white, and red fly on poles all around. The man stands near this vast common.

 "Monsieur Vizir, I still do not have the answer. Are we who we think we are, or who we are proven to be?

I do not know. I am told that I am a great man. I am told that I suffered a nervous breakdown while living on Cul-de-Sac Ile. I am told I gave grandiose explanations on various topics to horses; I am told I engaged in puzzling, alarming conversations with other men of renown: marshals. I am told a veritable army awaits my arrival. And not just my arrival: my return."

The man stops in the middle of the plaza.

"I do not believe it. The evidence is overwhelming; a conspiracy so vast could never be executed. But I do not believe it. Yet if it is true, contrary to my own reflections, contrary to the drawers I would normally expect to find myself in, then I will continue my mission: spreading the word of the Organization—for it is a word that represents a noble Idea. A noble Idea I mean to live the rest of my life by. Passions change, Monsieur Vizir, but insurance ... insurance is immutable."

He continues toward the opposite edge of the square.

"Speeches pass away, sir, but acts remain. And my acts will better the citizens of the world, although my acts may not always make the people happier in the short run. After all, we must serve the people worthily and not occupy ourselves in trying to please them. The best way to gain their affections is to do them good. The Organization, insurance, that is what shall do them good, and that is what I will tell my army."

He stops midway between the center of the square and the opposite edge.

"I will tell them about unity. That our mission to fuse the world into one whole is right and just. I will tell them about loyalty. That we should not only follow the laws but that we should want to follow them. I will tell them about fraternity. That when we are unified, which can only be guaranteed by our loyalty, each and every man will be a brother to us, each woman a sister; and we will all be equal under this rule because we will know how to live life since it will be clearly outlined in constitutions we ourselves agreed upon; and although our choices shall be free, the world will be ensured to such an extreme that decisions will become obvious, danger will be scarce, nonexistent. I will tell them about all of this. I will tell them about insurance."

The man reaches the opposite edge of the square, pats his horse on the neck.

"And, Monsieur Vizir, our cry will be, 'With the Organization: Honor, Glory, and Riches Are Yours.' Honor, Glory, and Riches."

From the edge of the square, a tumult is heard, as if a crowd were assembled on the other side of the building the man faces. He adjusts his black bicorne hat, brushing the flourish of color at the peak. He smooths his blue uniform. And, according to the tutelage of Monsieur Talma, according to the precepts of Aeschines, he places his hand between the second and third buttons of his waistcoat. Then he proceeds forward with masculine style and grace, like a Roman senator, to meet the masses.

BASTILLE DAY

for Megan Milks

It is Tuesday, July 14, and it is raining. He knows it is Tuesday because the plastic pill compartments for both Sunday and Monday are open, and empty. Perhaps the days all seem the same, but the pills in their compartments tell him that at least time is progressing. Then time finishes and starts over. Another week. A progression in cycles. He knows it is raining because he can hear water droplets on the windows. He cannot hear them hit the roof because the roof is six floors up. He cannot see the water droplets because the blinds are closed. He will not move to open them. The fact is negligible at any rate. Or is it? July 14 is more difficult to prove. If he had a newspaper, the date could be ascertained if he trusted the source. And knew it was today's paper. It could be yesterday's or last week's. You see where this is going. On the table is a copy of *White Noise* by Don DeLillo, opened to the twenty-fourth page, where characters discuss how one knows when it is raining. Our character looks from the twenty-fourth page to the pill compartments and wonders if he remembered to take his pills yesterday. If he forgot, then today might be Wednesday. If he forgot two days running, or three, or four, it could be any day. If he accidentally took his pills twice one day, despair. Every year in July, he reads *White Noise*, though not by design. This year it has possibly taken him fourteen days to reach page twenty-four, where there is a discussion about how one knows when it is raining, which makes our character wonder if it's actually raining, or if someone is throwing pebbles against the windows, or if a tree's branches are brushing the glass in just such a way, or if he can trust his hearing or mind at all—did he forget to take his pills? The pill compartments suggest it is Tuesday, making it July 14. If it is July 14, our character thinks, then many years ago in France, supposedly, there was a prison break. He imagines there must've been a good reason for it but can't think of what that reason is. Or was. Then, he assumes, being in prison is probably a perfectly good reason to have a prison break. There is a tapping sound at the window. The twenty-fourth page of *White Noise* says, "A victory for uncertainty, randomness, and chaos." The pills, trapped in their compartment, wait.

LIFE INSURANCE

> Building the towers belongs to the sky,
> When the whole thing comes crashing down,
> don't ask me why.
> —Soundgarden, "Limo Wreck"

Woke up in the hospital, and They told me I'd been legally dead for three minutes. So, I had to fill out the Death Certificate. Filled out the Death Certificate, but since I was alive again, They told me I was gonna have to fill out the Resurrection Certificate. Only They said I shouldn't go fillin' it out right away on account of my boss was gonna fire my ass 'less I was officially, authentically, certifiably, approved dead. They said I oughta go on down to the funeral home, make the preparations so's I could keep my job. Wunnered what a dead man needed with a job, but I went anyway. At the funeral home, Undertaker asked me if'n

I wanted to be buried or burned. When I said burned, Undertaker told me that'd be fifteen hundred bucks. ... Said I left my checkbook out in the car. In the car, I started her up and roared outta there. Figgered: if I've got three days' funeral leave, I ain't wastin' it with the Undertaker.

On the way back to my place, cop wearin' mirrored sunglasses pulled me over for doin' hunnert-and-five in a thurdy-five. He asked me: "You know how fast you were driving, sir?"

"One hundred and five miles per hour," says me.

"That's correct, sir. Why were you driving so fast, sir?"

"I've got three days' funeral leave. Wanted to get back home."

"Funeral leave, sir? Who died, sir?"

"I did."

"You did, sir?" he said, all sarcastic-like.

"Yeah, look." Got out the Death Certificate and handed it over.

"How did you die, sir?"

"I don't rightly know. Just woke up this morning, and They told me I was dead."

"'They,' sir?" says the cop, archin' an eyebrow over them mirrors. "Who are *They*?"

"The hospital people, I guess."

"I see, sir."

Cop scratched his head, and I pointed to the Death Certificate. He made sure it was signed by all the appropriate people, asked me if that was my signature at the bottom: I swore it was. Cop said it's not polite to swear, and I wunnered what it mattered, seein' as how I was dead. Then he took out a red rubber stamp, after checkin' the piece of paper three, maybe four times, askin' each time if that was my signature at the bottom and not someone's I was pretendin' to be dead for, and settin' the piece of paper on top of my car, he gave it a good stamp.

"I pulled you over because you were driving too fast, sir. And the police are here for your protection, sir." Cop tried to smile after this, then kept talkin'. "But we're also here to keep some sense of authority, and the only way most people ever feel our authority is when we pull them over for speeding, sir. It reminds them that we're here, sir. That we're keeping the peace and keeping our jobs intact, sir. ... Well, enjoy death, sir. But try not to drive so fast. You're liable to get yourself killed."

Took a gander at the Death Certificate. Had a red stamp that said OFFICIAL. So now, I was officially dead —which felt nice. And with thoughts of a parade and a ceremony for bein' declared "officially" dead by the *police*, cranked my car back up to 105 miles per hour and headed back to the ranch.

Back at the ranch, which's actually my apartment, noticed the light on my answerin' machine was blinkin' like as if it was 'bout to explode. Pushed the button, machine said, "You have a hundred billion messages," in this creepy, metallic voice with all this screamin' and groanin' in the background to make ya think it was recorded in hell or some such place. Then the thing up and died in a puff a smoke. Figgered I was gonna have to pick up a Death Certificate for that there machine.

LIFE INSURANCE

But since it was dead and m'trumpet was leanin' nearby, felt it'd be good of me to play "Taps" in honor of the departed, so to speak.

Tried to play "Taps," only when I picked up the trumpet, damn thing rusted through and fell apart, meanin' it was dead, too—another Death Certificate. Gave up on playin' "Taps," so's I decided to bow in rev'rence to the passin' of my phone message machine and m'trumpet, rest their souls. Then tried to turn on the TV, but with a snap-hiss, it joined my message machine and m'trumpet in that Big Scrap Heap in the Sky.

Them weren't the only things to go. Found that all the food in my 'frigerator was spoilt on account of the coolin' system went down, and none'a the lights in the place would turn on without the bulbs explodin' a second later, and when I tried to light my last cigarette with the flame from the stove, stove gave a loud bang and fell to a heap on the ground. Another heap. Pictured me a big ol' heap'a them Death Certificates and wunnered if I oughta go into the Death Certificate printin' bidness. Make me a killin'.

So's I sat down on m'couch, which the legs promptly fell off of, crashin' me an' the couch to the floor. Thought about maybe lookin' into a new apartment when the phone started ringin'.

Person on the other end said, "Have you thought about life insurance?"

I said, "Life insurance?"

"Life insurance, sir. You never know when an accident might take you away, leaving your loved ones in financial ruin."

Pieces'a plaster from m'ceilin' took to fallin', hittin' me in the head as I sat on the couch, talkin' to the salesman. "Tell me there, feller."

"What can I assist you with, sir? I would be happy to help you in any way possible."

"You think maybe someone named yours truly on their life insurance? Because I seem to be in financial ruin." Plaster took to pourin' off of the ceilin' now, landin' in a heap on the floor, 'long with big ol' pieces'a wood that were crashin' to the ground with me runnin' all over hell's half acre, or at least hell's five-hundred square feet, tryin' to dodge all that there debris.

"I'm not sure, sir."

Tossed the phone in the corner, jumped for the door—had to jump on account of a big hole just opened up—and with a crash, slammed shoulder-first into the hatch, knockin' it open, spillin' myself out into the hall. Tore outta the buildin', wunnerin' the whole way if mayhaps I oughta tell the landlord 'bout all this. Only I didn't have to think about it long 'cause he was standin' right out front, and me and him watched the whole goddamned place come tumblin' down. In a heap. Of course.

Landlord looked at me, said, "You having any problems with your apartment?"

Glanced over at the heap, then back at the landlord. "Gotta jiggle the handle on the toilet, but otherwise there's only this ..." says me pointing at the wreckage.

"Good. Rent's due tomorrow."

"Rent?"

There were a loud crash.

"*Tomorrow.*"

"Might be late."

"Why's that?"

"I'm dead."

LIFE INSURANCE

Back in m'car, out on the road, suddenly m'engine up and dies. Only it wasn't really dead, just run outta gas. Right outside a Presbyterian church (maybe I'll go in an' give thanks for not needin' a Death Certificate for my motor) located between the towns of B.F.I. and B.F.E. Git this: This here church didn't have any foundation, and there's a little hill in the middle of the bottom, like as if to make you think two people jumpin' on opposite ends would send the whole place a teeter-totterin'. Figgered the preacher'd give me a ride, though, so I let m'self in.

Was the only person on the inside, so's the whole place slanted in my direction. Luckily, everything seemed to be bolted down. Then, like a bat outta hell, the preacher jumped an' landed on the podium, sendin' the whole place slantin' in his direction, me tryin' to hold onta anything at all but havin' a devil of a time till I was 'bout halfway down the aisle, where I was able to grab hold'a couple pews in the pose'a that there Jesus fella, praise his name.

"Have you thought about your life, sir?" the preacher asked.

Mentioned that it'd crossed m'mind a time or two, only I didn't bother with it too much. Naw. "Anyway," says me, "I'm dead."

Now the preacher, he's right at the end of m'slant, so's if I let go'a them pews, I'd slide right to the base'a his podium like as if to make me think I'd skid to perdition, him lookin' like the angel of vengeance or fire or some such.

"Life is not funny, sir! Especially yours. It is tragic. Tragic! You are spiraling toward an all-encompassing spiritual demise, and there's nothing you, alone, can do about it. You must prostrate yourself before the Almighty, give yourself to His mercy. The mercy of God!"

Preacher'd worked hisself up into a fury, words ringin' off the walls, round face all red, eyes burnin' through me, arms above his head to make ya think if he dropped 'em, the floor'd disappear, and a bottomless pit'd swallow yours truly.

Blinked up at the preacher and said, "Padre, all I want's a ride so's I can pick up some gas. Ran out in front of the church."

"All you want is gas?" He looked up. "All he wants is gas, he says! But little does he know that death looms around the corner. Ever-present, omnipotent death, where no life for his kind exists. What are you going to do, sir? What are you going to do when the good Lord decides that it is your time to go?" Started pointin' at me again, leanin' over the podium.

"Sign the Death Certificate, Padre," and I let go'a them pews, slid all the way to the podium, stood up, set the piece'a paper in front of the preacher, who put his readin' glasses on, an' pronto!, that changed his whole deal, see, from the fire-and-brimstone man'a God who scares the bejesus outta you into a guy who might issue you a new driver's license, or better yet, a library card.

Reverend Books said, "I see. Is this your signature?"

So … said it was. Preacher went over my Death Certificate three, maybe four times, each time askin' if'n that was my John Hancock, so to speak, at the bottom'a the page.

LIFE INSURANCE

Said, "Do you think I'd pretend to be dead for someone else, Padre?"

Preacher assured me he's just makin' certain, then he pulled out a blue rubber stamp and stamped my Death Certificate. "I accosted you at the door because my job is to get people to think about their lives. But mostly I scare them with ghost stories about the devil and hell. Those stories keep the contribution plates full, and they happen to entertain me, too. ... So, make sure you follow the Ten Commandments or else you'll end up *you know where*." Here, he briefly turned back into the prophet. "And enjoy your death, sir."

He left out the back, leavin' me standin' there, Death Certificate in hand.

Looked at the Death Certificate, saw next to the red OFFICIAL stamp it had a blue CERTIFIED stamp. Officially, certifiably dead. Seemed too easy. Always had problems with paperwork. Only I didn't complain. What I did do: jumped to the middle of the church and just balanced there for a while. Like as if I was the center'a the merry-go-round. You gotta do stuff like that every now an' then ta remember you're alive.

Even when you're dead.

Had to walk all the way to the gas station, passin' more garbage heaps than I'd ever seen before, thinkin' they used to be apartment buildings. Some of 'em I even watched fall right to the ground. Only I was gittin' kinda used to it. Kinda excitin'. And hell, they bring the offices to you when you die, so's I think I like bein' dead plenty better than bein' alive. Got my Death Certificate stamped twice without havin' to go stand in any long lines where'n they tell ya, "Naw, you want t'other line, not this un," then ya get over to the other line, and they say, "Naw, you want that line you just stood in where'n they told ya to come over here. Only that line's closed now."

Death Certificate bidness, though, ran like a charm.

Got to the gas station, said, "Need a gas can, couple gallons'a gas, pack'a cigarettes."

Lady rang up the can, gas, no cigarettes.

"Need cigarettes, too," says me.

Lady shook her head. "Cigarettes'll kill ya, you know?"

Said, "I know. I'm already dead."

Got out my Death Certificate, lady laughed (figger everyone deals with death in their own way), said something 'bout how I was CERTIFIED and OFFICIAL, and she asked if'n that was my signature at the bottom. Checked to make sure I hadn't mixed up my certificate with somebody else's 'long the way, but it was mine all mine. Just like the cop and the preacher, she checked it over three, maybe four times. I checked it, too. After the whole ordeal, got out a green stamp, and she slammed it down on the piece of paper. Sound made me kinda proud. Like I'd accomplished something.

Lady said, "I'm only here because I can't find another job, and frankly, I couldn't care less if the whole place went up in flames. But I need the money, and I'm too lazy to go anywhere else, so I stay here. … Anyway, all the stuff is free for the deceased today. So, enjoy your death, and stop smoking cigarettes. Those things'll kill ya."

"Says you," says me, and I left the store with an OFFICIAL, CERTIFIED, and APPROVED Death Certificate. Wonder if that'll git me a discount at the grocery store like the old folks get.

Finally got back to m'car with the gas. Stayed away, though, on account'a I saw two guys fightin' over a fenderbender near where I was parked. All's I could hear was:

"I'll kick your ass."

"Well, I'll kick your ass."

"I've got a knife."

"I've got a gun."

"I've got a grenade."

"Me, too."

Jumped into a ditch outside the church, heard two explosions, then three others. First two were grenades. Three others were cars. Walked over to where m'car had been, only now it was a heap. Realized the gas weren't gonna do me no good. Like everything else. To prove them all wrong, thought real long and hard about chugging some'a that fuel, just tiltin' the can up and suckin' the juice down, makin' it look all refreshin' like as if this were a TV commercial for a new drink, "Octane will git ya goin' and keep ya goin' for miles," or some such. I mean, what could it hurt since I was dead an' all, but for reasons I can't rightly explain, I didn't do it.

Then, I saw the heaps of the other two cars. Nothin' worked on them, either. 'Cept fer one thing: cell phone was ringin'.

Why not?

Answered the phone thinkin' 'bout Death Certificates for both of them thar grenade lobbers and the three cars and wunnered just who in *the* hell was gonna fill out all'a them Death Certificates, how They ever have enough time for 'em all. Or if maybe there were *en*-tire rooms full-up with not-filled-out Death Certificates just waiting to be claimed by the folks who fill Death Certificates out. Then I got to wunnerin' 'bout who fills out Death Certificates in the first damn place on account'a I don't remember seein' anyone fill mine out, when the voice on the other end said, "Have you ever thought about life insurance?"

Said, "What?"

"Life insurance, sir. You never know when you might pass on due to some senseless act of violence, leaving your loved ones in financial ruin."

"That's the Lord's truth," says me. 'Cept I hadn't seen no Lord. Which made me wunner if somewhere there were a monumental heap, like the biggest of all time, an' from just the right distance, naw, keep goin', further, further!, yeah, yeah!, see?!, it's obvious: You-know-who took a header and fell right outta the sky.

I wunner who signed *that* Death Certificate. …

Figgered I needed a drink, so's I decided to swing by m'brother's bar, which weren't too far off. Whole way there all's I could think 'bout was how much I liked bein' dead better than alive. Didn't have to go to work. Didn't get speedin' tickets. Didn't have to pay rent.

Didn't have to deal too much with preachers. Free cigarettes.

Bar was full-up with people, so's I sat in a booth in the back waitin' for it to thin out.

Guy sits down across from me, says, "Can I ask you a question?" Spoke like he's makin' sure he said all them words right. Guy was dressed up in gray and wearin' sunglasses.

"Shoot."

"How was your day?"

"Pretty strange."

"Why?"

"Welp, let's just say I'm officially, certifiably, approved dead. Wanna know the damnedest part?"

"What?"

"It's the greatest thing in the world."

"Interesting." Guy seemed all interested in this. "Can I see your Death Certificate?"

So's I got out my Death Certificate, slapped it down on the table.

He picked it up. Guy looked at it, said, "Have you ever thought about life insurance?" Guy got out a briefcase I didn't see him carry in, opened the golden latches that made this sound like a sledgehammer hittin' a spike. Looked at me ... then looked inside his briefcase.

"Who are you?" says me.

"I am the Authenticator. Now, can I interest you in life insurance?" Pulled out a policy and a pen, poised a black stamp over my Death Certificate.

I looked over at m'brother standin' off in the distance.

Guy said, "You never know when you might *disappear from the face of the earth without a trace,* leaving your loved ones in financial ruin." Paused for a second there.

I said, "Yeah … so, uh, right, maybe you oughta sign me up for some'a that, uh, life insurance, or what have ya."

"Indeed," and he handed me a pen.

Got all cold in the bar, and I started to sweat, and the lights got all dim an' I couldn't tell if I was signin' or not when m'brother tapped me on the shoulder.

"Hey, bro," he says. "Didn't even know you was here. Anyway, They brought this down for ya earlier."

Only I weren't real sure that was m'brother, and I weren't real sure I was in the bar cuz I weren't real sure 'bout anything right then 'cept I got this vision: Was a big ol' factory, all shiny like as if it were brand new, only ya got the idea that it weren't new at all, an' it was so damned huge ya couldn't really see the top, 'cept you could see all the black smoke 'cause the black smoke was the clouds. Fact'ry made so damn much noise it was like yer heart beatin' after bein' chased by a tiger or some such thing, an' then some joker up an' stuffed your heart right in yer ear, an' on one end'a the fact'ry, trees went in, an' on t'other end, Death Certificates came out, just churnin' 'em out from some forest so full-up with trees They weren't ever gonna run low, an' it always looked the same no matter how much time went by, an' it prints them thar Death Certificates night an' day an' day an' night, an' I'm standin' right out there in front of it, an' I walk up an' grab me one'a them pieces'a paper. One of them Death Certificates. An' on the back: why, if it ain't a life insurance policy.

"Look," and m'brother opened the envelope.

Suddenly I was all sure 'bout everything. Least as sure as I used to been. Brother was holdin' m'Resurrection Certificate.

LIFE INSURANCE

I turned to the salesman, said, "Don't think I'll be needin' any life insurance today."

"I see," and the guy took the policy and the pen and the stamp and put 'em all away. Then he stood up, headed out, still not carryin' the briefcase I didn't see him carry in.

Stopped the guy before he left. "Hey, you want this?" Held up my Death Certificate.

"No, we have plenty. And we can make more." Then he was gone.

Turned to m'brother, who sat down across from me.

Says him, "Bro, it's been a rough day."

"Bet my day was worse," says me.

"Why's that?"

"I died."

Brother laughed, said I might want to get my Resurrection Certificate stamped down at the office. Didn't say which one. Didn't say who I might need to see. Didn't tell me which line to stand in. Don't think I'm goin' to any office, anyway. 'Cause if I did, all's I'd think 'bout is when the whole mess'd come tumbling down, Death Certificate printin' office and all, in one resoundin' crash, endin' in one astoundin' heap. Figger my Death Certificate'll be signed, stamped, and filed long before that there demolition. Which is fine by me. Have enough problems with the minor collapses. Let alone the biggest one.

AN IMMATERIAL MESSAGE

That worthless pothead, your roommate, so the rumor runs, has sent a message to you, the strait-laced student, the tired-of-staying-up-so-late-every-night-because-someone-won't-let-you-go-to-sleep guy snoozing on the other side of the room, the pothead from his miniature den of iniquity has sent a message to you alone. He has commanded, or at least asked nicely in his confused sort of way, for the messenger, his girlfriend, to lean closer to him as they both recline in bed and has whispered the message to her; so much store did he lay on it that he repeated the message two or three times. Then, by a nod of the head, the girlfriend confirmed that she had no clue as to which message to deliver because, having repeated the message two or three times, the pothead had, indeed, communicated two or three different messages with nary a similarity between them. And since there was no one else, no one of import anyhow, to hear the message in your cramped, cluttered, claustrophobic dorm room, only the girlfriend knows the words your stoner roommate spoke. Never can the girlfriend deduce the actual meaning of the message because of the disparate communications and because she herself is trashed; hence, she would have had trouble comprehending a clearly stated message that had been repeated verbatim several times. Yet, what does get through to this messenger is the fact that something (whatever it is) must be delivered to you. Oh, but the journey is so far! So arduous! For in order to deliver the message, first the girlfriend must lift herself from the bed—and that is not all. If that were all, perhaps, *perhaps* she could make it. But no. Even if she were able to stand, she would then have to right herself, to gain and retain her balance, for in the likelihood that she lost her balance, she would collapse to the floor, and then she would never rise again. Yet, should she remain upright, her journey would still be impossible, for still there would be the task of scaling the pile of dirty laundry directly next to the bed, and that pile is insurmountable: It can never, never be passed. If someone *could* climb that pile of laundry, and that someone is certainly not the messenger, such a person would next have to rappel down the various stacks of aluminum cans, which stretch on forever. Beyond the cans are the fast-food wrappers, the assorted textbooks covered in maple syrup and Chili Cheese Fritos, the broken jewel cases for unknown CDs, the treacherous strands of beads hanging from the ceiling, the "We're Number One" foam-rubber hand with the middle finger extended. The worthless pothead's girlfriend must get past all of this. And she has yet even to stand up from the bed. But still, on the other side of the room, maybe ten or fifteen feet away, you sit and wait.

THE COMMITTEE FOR STANDING ON SHOULDERS

When the bar first opened, back in the early hours, everything was going fine. Or so they say. I'm not exactly sure I was here for the opening, when they cracked the doors for the first time, but if I wasn't around when the doors opened, I was sure as hell here soon after. 3Orb—when I first got here, anyhow—was a great place. It was spacious. Comfortable. Relaxed. Not like now. Now, we've got people to the ceiling. And since 3Orb's outside the fire code, more and more people get let in. Can't go hurtin' anyone's feelings. So, even though someone ought to've up and said, "Nah, we can't fit no more inside," they keep pouring through the doors. We'd complain to the bartender, but he stepped out some time ago, and ain't no one's seen him since.

The bartender, well, he's the bartender and the owner. In the early hours, right after I arrived, someone asked the bartender why he named the place 3Orb. Only, as it turns out, he didn't name the place anything. His dishwasher named it 3Orb. Said that'd bring plenty of people in on account of they wouldn't know what to expect out of it. Is it a bar, a nightclub, a coffeehouse with alcohol? No one would know until they came in. And plenty of people came in, so I guess the dishwasher was right.

Before everyone started rushin' in, gushin' like millions of gallons of water, you might say, you could look all around. The early atmosphere was pretty light. You could see the other side of the place with no problem. You could see the jukebox, the tables and chairs, the fish tanks (I guess the bartender likes fish), the dartboards, the pool tables, the plants, and even the high ceilings painted blue with fake clouds. You could see the limbo rod, too. He never said, but we figured the bartender wanted to have some old-time limbo competitions, see just how low we could go. Whatever the reason, it was a really nice limbo rod, painted a bright red. Back previous to all the people showing up, you couldn't help but stare at that rod and wonder what the bartender planned to do with it. If anything. Maybe he just liked the way it looked. In them early hours, quite a few people liked the way it looked.

No one expected the limbo rod to become an idol, but it did.

Yeah, in 3Orb. Having a good old time. Not too many people. Just a few of us. Listening to the jukebox.

Talking to each other. Some people playing darts. Some people shooting pool. Others sittin' there enjoying their beer and pretzels. You had to get your own pretzels from a big old bin that sat to one side of the bar, but they were damn good. So, no one minded. At least, that's the way I remember it bein'. It might be that we're so gosh-darned hungry right now we'd eat any old pretzels, even if someone stomped on 'em and ground 'em up into their shoes. That might be why we remember them pretzels tasting so good. The beer we had to drink, well, it was home brewed. The names of the beers were colors: Red, Yellow, Blue, Green. That's all we had, but it was all right.

The problems started with the night crowd. Guess the word got around about 3Orb, or maybe the dishwasher was right, and everyone was all intrigued by the name, meaning they couldn't resist. So, when the night crowd got to pouring in, gushing in, well, no one bothered to take a count of how many people were sloshing through the doors. We were outside of the fire code. Let everyone in. Everyone and his brother. Nah. Tell 'em to leave their brothers at home. Nothing worse than a bar filled with dudes and no women. Bet anyone would agree with that.

In a matter of minutes, 3Orb got to be pretty lively. People yakking throughout the place with a whole mess of ideas, some good, most bad, a few terrible, and one or two probably genius (promptly ignored until it was too late). Then, as more people arrived and someone turned up the jukebox, the place, well, it was rockin'. There was music and people chattering and people dancing and people drinking beer, eating pretzels (plenty of pretzels back in the early hours) and people playing pool and people throwing darts. The hubbub was mighty interestin', and the whole time the bartender just stood there and smiled a little, happy smile and didn't say a word. He pulled the taps whenever someone ordered a beer, and that was it.

Only the people didn't stop comin' in when we were rockin'. Nope. They kept flowin'. As more and more people poured in, 3Orb got to be pretty crowded. You might even say uncomfortably crowded. You couldn't walk across the bar to the restrooms without shoving people out of the way. Of course, that meant there were plenty of fights about to start all at the same time, and there were a bunch of barely avoided scuffles and all kinds of harsh words shouted back and forth, only people still couldn't hear one another, so the words got misinterpreted and reinterpreted until no one had any idea what anybody else was sayin'. Even the people who weren't angry at someone for wantin' to make his or her way to the restroom were talkin' so much you couldn't hardly hear yourself think. There was just this constant buzz of noise like to make you think that you were sittin' in a whoppin' beehive, only it was people flapping their jaws, and no one could play pool anymore on account of folks dancing on the pool tables, and no one could play darts anymore on account of an untold number of fights that almost started or that did start on account of someone steppin' in front of one of them needle-points, and except for the people on the pool tables there weren't any room to dance in, either, and all the time the place was fillin' up more and more and more. Until 3Orb was—well, there ain't no other way to put it: swamped.

Somewhere around this time, the bartender disappeared. And you know what? That's really too bad.

THE COMMITTEE FOR STANDING ON SHOULDERS

Because it was just the time when we could've used him. Yeah, we knew we were outside of the fire code, but someone had to put a stop to all these people pourin' in. Pretty soon we'd be standing on one another's shoulders. Which is exactly what happened. About the time we were so crowded it was as if this were one of them soccer games over in England or Ireland where so many people all storm into the stadium and then some unfortunate folks, well, they get crushed. Maybe they get crushed and come out alive because someone's able to pull 'em out of the pile, or maybe they ain't so lucky. At 3Orb, we weren't so lucky. Or so the story goes. No one's exactly sure on account of there bein' so many people we really couldn't tell what was going on in general, let alone in specific. And when it got to the point where we really had no idea what was goin' on, and it was obvious that the bartender wasn't comin' back any time soon, we decided we needed a person or a group or something to figure everything out because all together we couldn't do it.

That's when we ended up with the Committee for Standing on Shoulders. They called themselves that, gave themselves that handle if you will, on account of their deciding that the best decision would be to get everyone to stand on one another's shoulders because there was certainly plenty of room up in the rafters, 3Orb having some pretty tall ceilings and all. But then, everyone demanded to know who would be on the bottom and who would be on the top. So, the committee, well, they decided that all of the really big, strong people should be on the bottom and that the average-sized people should be in the middle, and then the smallest people should be on the top. They figured that was the most logical answer.

Only the big, strong people, well, not all of 'em liked the idea of being on the bottom. They said they were being prejudiced against or what have you on account of their being so big and strong, and all of them shouldn't have to hold up the average-sized and smaller people. So, then, the committee decided that maybe there should be columns of big, strong people and columns of average-sized people and columns of small people, and they would all rotate around, so as to give everyone a chance at being a part of the different heights in the columns. And that sounded maybe even more logical than the first idea, although there was some concern as to whether some of the smaller folks could hold up an entire column, even if it was made of smaller folks, and then there were arguments about what made a person big and strong and what made a person average-sized and what made a person small, not to mention how pretty much nobody, no matter his or her size, wanted to be considered small. Other than that, it looked like we might give it a try.

Only there were plenty of folks in the various groups who said they shouldn't have to be on the bottom nohow, that they deserved to be at the top, and there were those who didn't figure they could hold one or two people, let alone an entire column. And everyone got to complainin', so the committee came to their decision, and they shouted, "Last one to the top is a rotten egg." This was certainly the worst idea the committee had come up with, but that didn't matter. Everyone immediately started crawlin' overtop of other people, and there were scramblin' folks all over the place makin' sure they got as far up as they could get, never thinkin' about how this was all pretty darned silly.

THE COMMITTEE FOR STANDING ON SHOULDERS

When the columns got set, it was pretty funny to hear the various folks talk because you'd think someone who knew about these kinds of things had come in and ordained where each and every one of us should be. The people up at the top, well, they were positive that they belonged up at the top, and strangely enough the people down on the bottom kind of figured they were supposed to be on the bottom. But the people in the middle, well they didn't much care for their placement. Most of 'em thought they were supposed to be up at the top, that there'd been this great big mistake in the masterplan, as if there had been any plan at all, and that if people would only give a listen in their direction, everyone would see why the middle folks ought to be up where the top folks were. No hard feelings, just let us up. Only the top folks wouldn't have any of it, and so they had a mighty enjoyable time watchin' the middle folks try to scamper to the top, sometimes actually makin' it, sometimes messin' up so bad that they ended up on the bottom, but most of the time stayin' right where they started, all frustrated and such.

Since the bartender was gone, the people on the bottom, who had been talkin' about him from the beginning, sayin' *he* ought to be the one who did the decidin' (even though we pointed out that he was nowhere to be found), started lookin' to the limbo rod for guidance. They took to sayin' we should all look to the limbo rod, and if we would only look to the limbo rod, then we would see what we were supposed to do, on account of the limbo rod would tell us, and then our problems would be solved. Now this sounded pretty crazy, but I guess after holdin' up a column of folks for who-knows-how-long, you tend to gaze beyond what's real, and there, in the baloney fields, you see a glorious solution to all your problems. Even the middle people got a little touched, especially those who were all the time tryin' to get to the top, and they sought out the guidance of the limbo rod, too, although I can't say that anyone ever really saw it do anything but sit there and be a limbo rod. The folks at the top, some of 'em feelin' kind of sorry for the schmoes at the bottom, well, they looked over at the limbo rod themselves a couple times, but never really more than a couple.

All the time there was still this loud ringin', like as if you were sittin' in the biggest call center in the whole world, of everyone tryin' to talk all at once, and the committee was tryin' to do its job and make our tavern experience better. But mostly no one listened to the committee. It was just about impossible to get anything accomplished.

Right about that time—with the bartender gone and the jukebox broken and the pool tables havin' been crushed by so many people standin' on 'em, and all the fish bein' dead with the water drained out of the tanks by people who didn't think it was fair that they had to stand in fish tanks all wet just on account of that's where their columns were located, and the darts bein' used as weapons by people in the middle, and the cue sticks bein' used as weapons by the people on the bottom, and the cue balls bein' used as weapons by the people up top—right about that time, we ran out of pretzels and beer.

The uproar that came in response to that there announcement made you think you'd been sittin' in a library up until then, on account of everyone from the bottom to the top immediately demanded that the committee find a way to get us more pretzels and beer, and not in a couple hours—right now. All the time more and more and more people were comin' in, forming new columns, topplin' other columns, sometimes dominoing into next-door columns, so we were constantly buildin' up the old and knockin' down the new, and we didn't even have anything to eat or drink. But we were outside of the fire code, so who's to say how many people should be allowed in, and we don't want to hurt anyone's feelings because how would we look then? All prejudiced and such. So, we let 'em all in. Hell, bring your brothers, too.

And, you know, we'd've asked the bartender, who seemed like he might've been a decent guy (or maybe not, no one really knew him), but he must've heard about another bar that wasn't quite so crowded as his, or maybe he had another bar, or maybe after seeing all the people comin' into his bar, he decided that the bartendin' and ownin' business really didn't suit him all that well, so he'd handed the title over to some drunk sittin' at the end of the block and headed off into the night.

So, that's where we are now. There are columns in different states throughout 3Orb, and no one's listenin' to anyone else, and it's so loud with all the talkin' that the good ideas and the bad ideas get blended together, but we've got to say that it seems like only the bad ideas, the ideas the strong guys up at the top come up with, well, those are the only ideas that seem to get tried, and we don't have any pretzels, and we're all out of beer. And let me ask you, what's a bar without pretzels and beer? It's a darned sad place, if I do say so myself. Not to mention that we keep on crammin' more and more people in, and there's no sign of the bartender and everybody's unhappy, you might even say pissed, and the Committee for Standing on Shoulders, well, they themselves can't do anything at all about the situation. It kind of makes you wonder, as you hold some guy up who weighs twice as much as you do, while you're hoping that the column next door to yours doesn't fall over because people can get crushed in this place when them columns get to crashin' down, while you're kind of sick of the people in the middle scramblin' around all the time, while the people at the top act all important, tellin' us what to do, and the people at the bottom sound so stupid, sayin' they're where they're supposed to be because the limbo rod told them so, all of this makes you wonder when it's all gonna end.

And that's where I come in, on account of I have that knowledge. There's gonna be this big fight. Or maybe it'll be an accident. Or maybe the fight will come about by accident. Probably the smart people, who no one ever listens to, will predict exactly what's goin' to happen since they have all the evidence and know what to do with it. But no matter if it's a big fight or a mistake or an accidental fight or spontaneous combustion, with all of us inside, the bar will burst into flames. Flare right up into the sky. Maybe the people at the top will get to hollerin' and say this shouldn't be; maybe the people in the middle will feel even worse than usual; maybe the people at the bottom will say they knew this was coming all along, on account of the limbo rod told them so. It don't matter. 'Cause 3Orb will light up like a Roman candle. It'll burn to the ground with all of us inside. And since the bartender won't be here to help, to tell us what to do, we won't know where to go. We won't know how to handle the situation. Even the Committee for Standing on Shoulders will be baffled. And since we're outside of the fire code, the firemen will just stand around and watch 3Orb burn, while we scream and wonder how this could've happened.

THE DIVINE PLAN: NOTES FOR AN UNPERFORMABLE MISE-EN-SCÈNE

1. We open on blankness. Then, from the heavens, God steps down onto the empty stage. (If God prefers to leap onto the stage or float down to the stage, you'd better allow it because, you know, this is God we're talking about.)

2.
Now, this isn't an actor playing God, nor is it a faithful, realistic, or ironic portrayal of God; this is not the

stereotypical God with the white beard and the flowing robes; this is not an anthropomorphized God. This is the real thing. God.

3.
Much like the Supreme Court said about porn, you will know God when you see God. But you must search.

4.
And if it is found, in the search for God, that there is no God, then perform a different play.

5.
To find God, first try contacting the spirit of Bishop George Berkeley.

6.
Bishop Berkeley, after all, was one of the founders of empiricism, which states that "To be is to be perceived" (*"esse est percipi"*); he then said that a tree falling in the woods would make a sound even if no one was around to hear it because God perceives everything. Since perception, according to Berkeley, is required in existing, then Bishop Berkeley must have perceived God plainly, unambiguously, and would therefore make a good casting consultant.

7.
To contact the spirit of Bishop Berkeley, talk to a medium, for they can supposedly speak to the dead.

8.
Test your medium by pronouncing "Berkeley" like the California university, rather than how it's really pronounced—like Charles Barkley.

9.
If Bishop Berkeley cannot give you a clear, unambiguous description of God …

10.
… if Bishop Berkeley cannot tell you how to contact God …

11.
… then the project is wrecked, and you should despair at the bar farthest away from the stage where your play will not be performed.

12.
If it is found that the medium says Berkeley and not Barkley, if it is found that mediumship is just a scam, then the entire project is wrecked, and you should perform another play.

13.
Ideas on other plays to perform: *Waiting for Godot, The America Play, The Resistible Rise of Arturo Ui, Rosencrantz and Guildenstern Are Dead.*

14.
If you are able to find God, and you wish to perform this short play, you must begin by having God step out of the heavens onto the stage.

15.
You probably won't have to tell God to do so because God will already know what to do, knowing all.

16.
Give God some credit, would ya? Sheesh.

17.
After stepping out of the heavens, God will do the following: make a rock so heavy even God can't lift it, make a square that is a circle, make a movie starring Keanu Reeves wherein Mr. Reeves is actually able to play, convincingly, something other than a surfer or a pothead.

18.
God will then make a grand speech wherein God will explain what the divine plan is.

19.
God will not speak in prophecy, will not use parable, metaphor, or metonymy, will excise all abstractions, and, in a startling twist for God, will orate without ornament or ambiguity.

20.
If you feel up to it, you could give God a challenge by saying to God, "During your grand speech wherein you explain what Your divine plan is, You cannot use the sentence, 'I work in mysterious ways.'"

21.
But, in the end, such a statement, such a challenge would be unnecessary because God knows all.

22.
And God would let you know, mid-thought, not to worry yourself about giving God a challenge.

23.

And God would let you know without the use of language because God works in mysterious ways.

24.

In this play about God, you should know that the only proper pronoun to use in place of "God" is "God." This is extremely important, for the play is unperformable otherwise.

25.

When God is finished with his divine plan speech, next should come a dual performance, directly in front of God, of *Death of a Salesman* starring Marlene Dietrich as Willy Loman, Marlon Brando as Linda Loman, Divine as Happy Loman, and Keanu Reeves as Biff Loman, alongside *Long Day's Journey into Night* with Humphrey Bogart as Mary Tyrone, Elvis Presley (Vegas era) as James Tyrone, Max Schreck as Edmund Tyrone, Boris Karloff as Cathleen, and Keanu Reeves as Jamie Tyrone.

26.

See if the audience can tell the difference between the two plays, or if they bleed together.

27.

The only way to find out this information truly is by employing an equal number of psychics to audience members; the psychics will stand throughout the crowd and report what each audience member is thinking.

28.

You won't have to worry about whether the psychics are lying or not because you will inject them with sodium pentothal.

29.
On sodium pentothal, however, the psychics might admit to being not psychic at all.

30.
All of the above-mentioned deceased actors can be contacted via mediums ... maybe.

31.
Or God since you have God at your disposal.

32.
Keanu Reeves, however, can only be contacted by visiting him at the beach.

32a.
Or wherever he gets his weed, which may very well be the beach.

33.
But really anyone will do for the parts of Biff Loman and Jamie Tyrone because Mr. Reeves would not be convincing as either of them. Just ask God.

34.
God nods God's head.

35.
Overtop of the dual performance of *Death of a Salesman* and *Long Day's Journey into Night*, project three films: *Yojimbo*, *A Fistful of Dollars*, and *Last Man Standing*.

36.
The projectionist should use the rock that's so heavy even God can't lift it as a focal point for the three projectors.

37.
Only union projectionists should be used.

38.
Conduct a discussion about the similarities between the three films, about the differences. Then decide which is the best film by having a vote. In case of a tie, ask God.

39.
No, the vote is unnecessary. God already knows how it will turn out.

40.
God knew I would write this.

41.
And this.

42.
And …

43.
Turn the reins of the play over to God.

44.
When the director realizes that his play cannot be made, he walks out of the theater and gets on his bicycle.

45.
The director rides his bicycle through the rain.

46.
Simone Mareuil (again, the real deal, although she's dead) from *Un Chien Andalou* watches the director ride his bicycle down the road.

47.
What a nice day to ride a bicycle in the out-of-doors, actress Simone seems to say, but doesn't.

48.
Record this on color film.

49.
But because it's a black & white world, find that the film projects in black & white, which means mostly gray.

50.
The director continues to ride his bike, and he stops outside of a bar.

51.
In the bar, the director seems to say, "Why? Why? Why did God take over my play? Why didn't Bishop Berkeley warn me? Why didn't the mediums tell me that Bishop Berkeley was a sadist who liked to perceive people toiling away at impossible tasks? Why couldn't I have just been a surfer like Keanu Reeves?"

52.
But, actually, the director says nothing. He only seems to say the above by looking into his beer.

53.
Keanu Reeves comes into the bar wearing a nun's habit. He immediately takes it off in one motion as if it were a greatcoat.

54.
The director puts on the nun's habit and angrily leaves the bar.

55.
Outside, the director seems refreshed. He decides to ride his bicycle down the middle of the road.

56.
The director gets run over by a very old-fashioned car driven by someone long dead, but who can be contacted by a medium, God, maybe even Keanu Reeves.

57.
The director wonders why, why has this happened? Just when he's decided to go on and become what any sensible person would decide to become in this situation, he's been run down by a car.

58.
The director, by the way, had decided to become a pothead.

59.
Why, why? Could anyone give an explanation for this? Could God Godself explain the divine plan that includes this conclusion for the director? And it doesn't comfort the director, knowing that he doesn't have to ask these questions because God already knew that the director would ask them. And the director doesn't have to ask why God would let this happen, either.

60.
Because God works in mysterious ways.

A SKY PARTY

for Kate Lorenz

Now

Here, the abandoned warehouses are multiplying. They are not figuratively multiplying because warehouses, as a rule, are strictly literal. I tried to teach them about metaphor and simile, synecdoche and metonymy, but the material was beyond them. I told them there was an entire world beyond the world they knew. They didn't understand. I said one thing can mean one thing and at least one other thing. Quiet and humble, they reminded me that if one thing meant one other thing, too, then it wasn't one thing to begin with. It was two things. I said life isn't just crumbling bricks and shards of glass and urine-soaked hobos and oxidation. Think about what all those things can mean, what they can symbolize. The warehouses were confused. I tried to explain more, but they said no, no, no, *oxidation*? I said oxidation is rust. Rust, they knew. Rust is reality.

Then

The First Woman I Ever Met from Kansas said she was from Kansas but didn't say where in Kansas. She just said, you know, Kansas. As if Kansas and I were acquainted. As if the two of us went way back. Nice to see you again, Kansas, it's been a long time. How's Nebraska? Have you had any more problems with Oklahoma? Oh, you know, Texas will be Texas. I've heard it's best not to … I told her I didn't think I'd like Kansas much because I was a city boy, although I was already a man, but she didn't seem to mind my pretension at being younger. Really, I said, growing up in Norka (not giving a state since she didn't give a city), I was used to places that were made of cement, brick, asphalt, glass, and steel. I was used to places that were full of buildings and expressways and smoke.

But then the woman's head lazed back, and a languid smile spread across her face, and her eyes glowed as if she were recalling some exquisite ecstasy that was all hers whenever she wanted it. Her facial features went placid and smooth, and she said in a faraway voice, "But in Kansas … we have the sky … the most beautiful sky. …" As if overtop of every place else, there were only a faux-sky, a pseudo-sky, a poor copy of a poor copy of the real sky located over the great state of Kansas, my old pal.

And I thought to myself that it was best to avoid any place whose only selling point was the sky.

A SKY PARTY

Now

Walking the labyrinth of warehouses, I've come to know how they live. Mostly they lounge about in unsavory parts of town, hang out with industries that smoke long cigarettes (in this day and age), and end up stoned in blind alleys, unable to see they're crumbling in on themselves, unable to see they're falling apart. They have no delusions, only pure escapism. All they want is to get past the *now*. They try to forget the *then*, when they were useful. Politicians often mention the intervention of gentrification. Until that happens, or if it ever happens, the warehouses continue on—as the legislators talk and talk, amusing themselves with the many words they know that end with *-ion*. Traction. Detention. Depletion. Tension. Hesitation. Deceleration. Reduction. Pollution. Depression. Stagnation. Disintegration. Disorganization.

Then

I approached the Second Woman I Ever Met from Kansas this way:
"Hello, female."
"Female?" she said, angelic, smiling and laughing. Hers was an infectious smile, an infectious laugh—the agents of the Centers for Disease Control (CDC) had been trying to inoculate against it for years, formula upon formula, sixteen-hour days, seven days a week, no holidays, no sick leave, until finally ... But then, armed with their serum, they would meet her, and she would smile at them, and they would, no, can't, yes, they would smile back, and she, so kindly, oh, so kindly,

would ask them, if they wouldn't mind, if it wouldn't be a bother, to destroy those nasty vials, and the intrepid CDC agents, sixteen-hour days, seven days a week, no holidays, no sick leave, years and years, would happily, well, sure, of course, would happily comply, what, these vials? They couldn't possibly be important if *she* wants us to destroy them. ...

"Yes, female. That's you."

"Why 'female'?"

"Because there's no acceptable laid-back form of 'female.' Chick, broad, babe, toots, dame, even gal—they're all offensive or outdated. And so, you are female."

"What about for males?"

"The laid-back version is 'guy.'"

"But I can't just call you 'guy.'"

"Why not? That's my name. Guy," and I held out my hand.

Then

I know how the warehouses are multiplying. To alleviate their pain, they've taken up with one another. They use no protection. You know you can't teach an old warehouse anything. And they engage in their palliative. And in direct concordance with Lamarckian principles, which operate in the reproductive processes of storage facilities, the children are born decrepit, dilapidated, destroyed, dark. Exactly as their parents. Having no more horizontal room to expand, they've vertically integrated; they've stacked themselves to the sky, a Babel Tower not meant to illustrate the greatness of man, not meant to challenge the grandiosity of God—instead a titanic accident, accident on top of accident, for which, should the warehouses or the neighboring human beings be taken to task for this sprawling, ever-expanding structure, should God ask what, indeed, we meant by this mammoth melancholic edifice, we would certainly apologize and slink back to our blind alleys. But those blind alleys would not be our blind alleys. They would be different blind alleys. For all the roads here are blind. And you can never find where you're going. You can't find who you're looking for. You can't see more than twenty feet down any road without the view being interrupted by an apologetic abandoned warehouse. And, should you turn your eyes to God to ask why, you'll find …

You can't see the sky.

Then

The Second Woman I Ever Met from Kansas shook my hand, laughed at my lame joke, laughed at any joke, laughed and smiled the whole time, and I didn't want to see the end of the smiles.

"Well, if you get to be Guy, then I get to be Girl."

"You mean 'grrrl.'"

"Don't growl at me," she said, with more laughing.

"Where are you from, Girl?" not yet knowing that she was to be the Second Woman I Ever Met from Kansas.

"Kansas," she said. And I thought to myself that perhaps there were no towns in Kansas, that the people who lived in Kansas were so laid-back, so relaxed, that they didn't need that uptight naming system. Just *Kansas* was good enough for them.

"Kansas," I repeated, and somehow her smile got bigger, as she fiddled with her straw. "I met a woman once who told me that what she liked about Kansas was the beautiful sky ..."

(Girl's eyes began to glow.)

"... and I wondered about a place where the only selling point was the sky."

Girl's features went placid and smooth, and her voice sounded as if it came on a special wind from the plains. "The sky ... the most beautiful sky. ... You can see ... Forever."

But you can still smoke in the bars here, so I couldn't tell that the *F* was capitalized. "Well ..."

Her original smile returned, only now there was something numinous about it. "In Kansas we have sky parties. We lay on the ground and hold hands and look ... look at the beautiful sky ... the most beautiful sky. ..."

I was getting creeped out; I thought maybe Kansas was a cult. So I asked, "Uh ... so how long will you be here for?"

Now

In an attempt to explain metaphor to the warehouses, I invent a story about meeting two women from Kansas. The warehouses understand what I mean when I say *women*. They understand that the first is there to set the scene for the second. They understand Kansas: a flat state in the center portion of the U.S.A. They even laugh at some of the jokes. But the warehouses take the story at face value. They don't understand when I say it can mean something else, too. And they certainly do not believe that the story has been fabricated. The warehouses say that I'm just like them—why won't I admit it?

THEN

Her smile was a knowing smile. "You can come with me."

"Where?"

"To Kansas. And we can go to a sky party. And we can lay on the ground and hold hands and kiss. And maybe we can even give you a real name. And I'll tell you my real name. And we'll have our real names, and we'll laugh, and we'll be happy underneath the beautiful sky. The most beautiful sky. You know you can see … Forever. In Kansas. So how about it?"

I said I didn't know, that I'd have to think it over, that I'd tell her tomorrow.

Her smile changed to the original smile and didn't change back. "Tomorrow the bars will be closed, and I will be gone."

"But tomorrow is Sunday. Why would the bars be closed on Sunday?"

"They say it was passed down from God."

"I guess you can't argue with that." We shifted gears. The rest of the night, Girl and I pretended we'd always been friends, since we were little children, since the beginning of time, and we created a history for ourselves, and in our history we were everywhere, went everywhere in the whole wide world, at every important historical epoch, everywhere except for Kansas. Our history was so vivid I thought it would go on forever. But the *f* was lowercase.

I don't remember how that night ended. But no matter the ending, I know the next day I expected the bars to be open, I expected to see her there in the same seat, and I expected our history to go on and on, into the future. But the next day, the bars were closed, and she was gone.

Now & Then

The warehouses are a difficult study. Their heads are full of the debris of painful memories cobwebbed together into a narrative they think of as reality, or at least a former reality, a parallel universe that they will never be able to reach or return to. If you question their Romantic absolute, they stonewall you.

Meanwhile, I move through the warehouses and use what I find inside, though normally entire floors, entire blocks are filled with garbage. And all the while, I keep trying to teach the warehouses that there is a metaphorical truth that can't be found in either pure escapism or absolute fact. But when I despair, when the warehouses seem too dense, too impossible, when I am weak, I give them the ending they want before I continue with my rummaging, the bittersweet ending that meshes with their sense of reality.

I say, "Sometimes I close my eyes, and I see a wide-open field and a group of people coming together in the wide-open field, and they all hold hands and lie down and look up at the sky, the most beautiful sky.

A SKY PARTY

You know you can see ... Forever. And I look down on them, as if I were some impotent god trapped up above, and I see Girl, and, no, not even to protect my vanity, I can't see myself there. The best (or worst) I can do is see her alone, one hand held by somebody, the other held by nobody, me, watching from above, wishing that someone would come down and take her hand, wishing that I were the one, but this is all a story, an invented history, so I watch the people down below, and their eyes glow, and languid smiles spread across their faces, their features go placid and smooth, and they experience the ecstasy of the firmament. Holding hands. At a sky party. In Kansas."

The warehouses say that *that* is the correct ending.

But it is not. And sometimes, when I see a rogue warehouse, off by itself, I whisper to it. I say that the Second Woman I Ever Met from Kansas comes back, that we run into each other here and there, and instead of me pining away for her, it's become obvious that she needs me, that the wide-open spaces are too wide open, and when we get together, whereas last time we talked about history, a history so devoid of absolute fact that Herodotus would have been scandalized (or maybe, he would've been proud), now and then we talk about science, philosophy, psychology, theology, communication, we talk about everything, we insert ourselves everywhere, but always Girl tries to get me to return with her to Kansas, where we will hold hands and kiss, and I will learn my real name at a sky party. But I am not going.

Once, though, I took her up to the top of the warehouse tower, and I showed her the sky from there.

She said, "This is not the beautiful sky I know."

"Of course not," I said. "It's the one that I know."

ASTRAY

An unlit cigarette dangled from my lips.

Outside, there was no one. Looking to the right provided a view of no one at all; looking to the left offered a scene devoid of people, while straight ahead was strictly unpopulated. There was no one. I lit my Chesterfield, and immediately a man asked me for a light. Normally, a person asking for a light already has something to smoke. Yet, he had nothing. His hands, which he clenched and unclenched, were empty. He sat down next to me, unperturbed at my immobility, and delivered this speech:

"I am the one who will lead you astray," he said, smoking, though I gave him neither cigarette nor flame. "I am the one who will lead you astray."

I looked down and found my own Chesterfield was missing. I removed one from the pack and lit it.

"I am the one who will lead you astray. There, I've said it three times, and what I tell you three times is true. So, you can believe it. Three times. You can trust me. It's true. Though, I only tell lies. I only tell lies. Lies, I must warn you, are all I tell. So, you can't trust me. You can't. You just can't. Not a blessed word," he said, taking a drag from the cigarette in his left hand, exhaling, and then taking a drag from the one in his right.

Meanwhile, I lit another.

"However, if you don't follow me, you'll never get to where you're going. Where you want to go. I am the one and only, the only one who can lead you to your destination. Your questions, the ones you want answered, will remain questionable, will remain querulous, will remain queer beyond your understanding if you stay here, if you follow someone else, if you allow me to walk into the distance shrinking—shrinking—shrinking until I am gone. Yes, if you do not join me, there will be no resolution for you; no, you will not get to where you need to go; no, you will not find that knowledge you wish to attain; no, you will not end up in the place you wish to be without me, though I," he said, inhaling on the two cigarettes in his left hand, slowly lowering that hand to his knee, exhaling, "I *will* lead you astray," punctuated by a drag from the righthand Chesterfield and a grand gesture with that same hand, sweeping the smoke away from his mouth.

I lit a fourth cigarette and ... handed it to him.

He thanked me and said, "Ah, but now I have said it four times, so we enter tricky territory. For: what I tell you one or two times is, let us be frank, a bald-faced lie; what I tell you three times is true; but what I tell you four or more times, you just can't tell, you just can't tell. I am afraid to inform you there is just no way to know," he said, inhaling from the two righthand cigarettes and the two lefthand cigarettes simultaneously, then exhaling, his hands in a flourish as if he were a conductor. "So, should you be ready, together we shall follow the path to your destination, a path only I know, a path only *I* can lead you along, though in doing so, inevitably, I will steer you off course and into oblivion." He stood and began walking.

I lit another cigarette.

I admit, I did not follow. I did not allow myself to be led astray. I watched him walk into the distance, ever into the distance, up to the point where the land meets the sky, just before he disappeared inhaling on the two cigarettes in his left hand, and then, with finality, the three others in his right, as he stepped over the horizon. It's been years since I saw him. And I wonder every day if I made the right decision. If perhaps my resolve to remain stationary was incorrect. If perhaps choosing to stagnate smoking on the stoop was wrong. If perhaps, in the end, my destination was to go astray, and I never made it, or if, after all, I am astray now.

A NAME YOU CAN TRUST

> Ah, Percivale, would ye fight with him? I see well ye have great will to be slain as your father was, through outrageousness.
> —Sir Thomas Malory, *Le Morte d'Arthur*

LINCOLN AND GOD
Of the hand of God, and how Lincoln came to meet the Missionary, and of other matters.

Perhaps *this* is what will happen. There will be a knock at the door. It will thunder against the oak, the only piece of true hardwood in the entire house (house?), reverberate off the Polaroid-covered walls: the walls painted a color unknown (blue? brown? gray? green?), based in lead, chips falling to the floor. The floor. The knock will resonate off the gray-tiled floor with a dull thud and then a rattle; the tile on the floor, the gray-tiled floor, will be worn, even more worn, beyond belief (but what is beyond belief? Can there be anything?), worn from years, yes, years (it won't seem that long) of people walking, pacing, plodding. Morose people. Desperate people. Angry people. Vengeful people. They will have worn the tile to a lifeless gray that no one bothers to clean; no one who visits will care. They will ignore the ill-lit room. They will walk quickly to the desk. The desk. The knock will shake the desk and everything on it. The desk will be black and made of metal; when kicked, the metal should indent, then pop out. It should sound like a bass drum. But it won't. There will be too many permanent depressions. On the desk, amidst a mound of miscellaneous debris, will be a toy: a ring of steel balls hanging from four strings; when the ball on the right is pulled and released, the one on the left should bounce out. No longer. One of the steel balls will be missing. They will swing chaotically from the force of the rap at the door. The rest of the debris: a broken green-hooded lamp, stacks of nickels and dimes with a postcard balanced atop (picture of a woman and a tree), an ashtray overflowing with Pall Mall cigarette butts, a mock diploma from a nonexistent school (the Laughing Academy), a small pizza box with moldy pizza inside, a three-quarters-empty bottle of Cutty Sark, a rusty helmet from a suit of armor, an ivory-handled Colt Single Action Army (SAA).

    The gun belongs to you. Lincoln. The man sitting behind the desk. Sleeping in your boxers and T-shirt. Feet resting in the pizza. Avoiding the knock. Willing it to go away. And although the rap won't be particularly loud, it will sound like the hand of God. To you.

A NAME YOU CAN TRUST

Actually, at the door will be the farthest thing from the hand of God: a Missionary. But you won't know that.

"Well," you'll mumble. "If God's coming to visit, luckily I'm looking my best." Thoughts of the past ringing in your head: a ruined castle, two birds (one white, one black), two chairs (one rotten, the other beautiful), serpents and lions (a whole menagerie), an entire evening of looking at Polaroids, Polaroids from the Winchester Riots and before, Polaroids arranged in a small square on the wall. It's unlikely that you'll be so coherent.

Rubbing eyes, brushing away ashes from half a cigarette extant from last night, wondering what the hell that smell is (sweat? lead? rotgut? plaster?), you'll swing your legs off the desk, find that they're still asleep, crash face-first onto the floor. You'll feel as if you'd fallen before. You'll figure it must not be a good time to wake up, laying your head back on a stack of old newspapers under your desk, trying to regain oblivion.

Yet the knock will come again. Louder this time.

"Shouldn't there be a bright light and a trumpet?" you'll mumble. But the only light, the desk lamp. And there won't be any music. Not now.

Covered in a fine layer of sweat, dirt, water (leaking pipes in the ceiling), and plaster (flaking down because of the leaking pipes), your face itches, so you'll scratch it and find a three-day growth that feels like rat hair. But there are no rats. Cockroaches. Everywhere. But no rats. Although it sounds like bullshit, rats really do leave a sinking ship. So, your life's become a cliché.

"All right, Lord. I'm coming," you'll say, rolling onto your back, immediately hit with another cloud of plaster. "I haven't found ... anything ... but I'm coming. Let's go, legs. It's time to meet God," you'll say, hands pounding against thighs, feet shuffling across paint chips—the best pair of shoes in weeks.

At the door, hand on the tarnished knob, best yellow-toothed smile in place, standing in the semi-dark, then ... on the other side, God will not be looming, overwhelming, casting judgment down upon you from some heavenly watchtower; instead there will be the sun, shining, an onslaught of light your eyes will refuse to accept, sending you again to the gray-tiled and paint-chipped floor. Your head will bounce with a hollow sound. The Missionary will almost drop his copy of *Lantern: A New Bible Translation*.

"My son, my son, you have fallen to the depths of *Hell*. Now, I am here to deliver you into the hands of the Savior," the Missionary will say, spittle inadvertently flying from his lips, embarrassment evident on his face that you'll miss because of the sun.

Shielding your eyes, consequently shielding everything, you will look up and say, "Tell me something."

"What would you like to know? The Lord answers all prayers."

"Does the savior ... does the savior have any Scotch?"

"Does the ..." An angry, fervid silhouette.

The Missionary will move in, so you can see him (at last): a middle-aged man; forty-five-ish; well-groomed gray hair; long, narrow face that comes to a point in an elongated chin; mouth large enough to fit an entire human fist. You'll look at your own fist, turning it in front of your eyes as you lay on the ground, but you'll decide the theory doesn't need testing.

"Alcohol is what has set you spiraling toward the infernal pits of the Abyss, son. Repent! Give up the devil's drink, and the Lord will accept you into His loving arms!"

"What? And give up all this?" You'll throw your arms up, sending paint chips scattering through the air. The helmet will fall off your desk.

"Son! You ... you ... The Lord can get you back on the right track. I swear to you, son: if you put your faith in the Almighty, you will be rewarded."

"Between you and me, padre, I hope I get rewarded with a bottle of Scotch."

LINCOLN AND HIS AUNT
How Joe Neminis met with Lincoln, and smote him down, and departed; and how Lincoln came to a recluse and asked counsel, and how she told him that she was his aunt.

The importance of a Polaroid is not in what it shows, but in what it doesn't show. What is remembered. What pictures the mental movie projector produces when prompted by the original image, the Ur-image. Here, in this particular Polaroid, the sun cracks through the clouds. Or is being covered by them. There is a shopping-bag woman standing at the corner in a bad part of town. There is a man whose face is obscured by light, by others, by commotion, pushing his way into the crowd. Leaving Lincoln in his wake. Lincoln lays prone on the ground. His left eye is swollen shut. All around, there are people breaking windows. Filthy water is backed up in the streets. Random fights rage. Fires burn. Inexplicable explosions. This is the picture.

Not in the picture:

Lincoln looked up, looked up in the direction of the man pushing into the crowd, the man's face blurry, even then blurry, an out-of-focus mystery, all a mystery. How had this happened? What had happened? The Winchester Riots, in full swing. All around. The Fraternal Order of Police had disbanded; the Winchester Police Department was in ruins; most of the cops were missing, or dead, or mercenaries waiting for the tumult to end, to subside, so they could exact their own form of costly justice, freelance justice. The riots had erupted after the downfall of the FOP and the WPD, after Mayor Ambrose Armathie was put in a coma, after Le Fey, the gangster, had taken Armathie's place as mayor, after Chief of Police Lance Malfet had disappeared. Now, there were only questions. For those who were left. For those who weren't rioting. Questions. Chaos. Blame replaced answers because there were no answers. Lincoln lay prone on the ground. Reaching toward his assailant. Remembering the beating he had taken from the assailant moments before. Too drunk to remember why the assailant would assail him. Remembering his brothers were killed in these riots by unknown hands. Remembering his father who died in the line of duty, one of the few good cops still around, who continued on after the others disappeared/got killed/left, who was positive that the corruption went beyond the known players, who was positive it could all be traced to one man, who was positive he could find that man, who was blind to all else except for who to blame. On the ground, Lincoln found who was to blame. For all of it. Much like his father.

Lincoln called to the shopping-bag woman. "Who was that?" asked Lincoln, struggling, unable to move much.

"Who? Dat guy? Joe Neminis?"

"That guy who dropped me? Joe Neminis?"

"Why?"

"Because I'm gonna kill him. I'm gonna hunt him down and kill him."

"Then you wanna croak like you pops."

"My father ... How do you know my father?"

"Cuz I'm yer aunt, sonny boy." The shopping-bag woman gave an awkward laugh. Wandered off. The sun was being covered by the clouds.

Lincoln and the Golden Idol
How Lincoln saw a client coming to him-ward, and how the lady told him of her disheritance, and how Lincoln promised her help.

Morgan Aurum walks into my office like she's strutting down a runway, and I'm holding a portrait of Madison. She's about six feet tall with heels, platinum-blond hair combed so it covers part of her face; her eyes are hidden behind black, thick-framed sunglasses. She doesn't want to see anyone but herself. We haven't said anything to each other, but I already know this: Early on, she was coaxed into believing her job was to send men off on pointless quests, to rob them while they were gone, to screw all of their friends for good measure. If the men were playing their parts right, they'd gallop out and labor for her happiness. Why? Because, according to the game, making her happy means you get the reward, the greatest weapon yet devised: her body.

Who could blame her for stepping right into the role she was supposedly born for?

"Are you Lincoln?" she says, sitting across from me.

I could blame her. "Do you only ask questions you already know the answers to? If so, I can just take a nap," I say.

"I was told you find people."

"Have you misplaced one?"

"I have someone who's missing."

"Careless. You should get a leash."

I've always been amazed by the detectives who say they don't do marriage work. Supposedly, the only cases they'll take are a family lamenting some wrong, or an individual seeking justice, or theft, or fraud, or the big one: murder. Maybe it's because Armathie's gone, Le Fey's running everything, and the FOP's in ruins, but all I get is everyone's dirty laundry. And they deliver it right to my desk. So, a detective who doesn't do marriage work just likes to sit in a dingy office drinking and smoking by himself.

Now that I think about it, maybe I *should* start turning down …

Morgan crosses her legs, makes her next play, starts singing her tune, a tune I've heard a million times before. It's called "Charity," and it comes at a hell of a price if you're not paying attention. It's like Lance always said, in this business, you better know all the songs. Because if you don't, if you lose sight of the conductor, you're liable to find yourself at the business end of a Saturday Night Special. And no matter who you are, you won't be able to face the music.

"Am I boring you, Mr. Lincoln?"

"Don't be so hard on yourself. I bore pretty easily."

"I could take my … *problem* elsewhere."

"Do it now. Go."

Pause.

"Still here? See, you could take your problem elsewhere. But you won't."

No matter how tough I sound, she can already see me running across town, the game afoot. You've gotten a piece, now run off, little boy, and if you're good you'll get more. More. There'd never be enough.

I say, "You're boring me because you're not speaking my language."

"And that is ...?" She recrosses her legs, leans forward; the music fades. What song is this? Whatever it is, I like it. Oh, do I like it. But this tune's not for me.

"Money," I say.

"Oh." She falls back in her seat. Maybe that image of her brainless knight traipsing across the city dims a bit.

I look her in the eye, tell her what I get paid. I feel like a wounded soldier bluffing his strength to an enemy. And hoping for surrender.

"That's pretty steep," she says. "Can I ... talk you down?"

Still staring into her eyes (sunglasses): "Nope."

She's used to getting her way. I'm used to being drunk by noon. People in hell want popsicles. If she keeps this fencing match up, I'm bound to lose. But, strangely, she gives in. An attack in itself since it's so unexpected. Like Lance says, the song ain't over just because there's a little quiet.

"Fine, I can afford your price," she says, sitting back, annoyed, a chink in her armor. Or maybe mine. "You better be as good as they say you are." She pulls a cigarette out of her purse, puts it in a black holder, starts smoking.

I smile. "Don't mean to boast ..."

"Then don't."

"… but I'm the 142nd best detective in Winchester."

She laughs, but quickly composes herself, pretending it's a cough. "What about Lance Malfet?" Morgan says. Another unexpected tack. How does she know about Lance?

"Well, you came to me. And no one's seen Malfet in years." I pull one of the steel balls on my desk gadget. It goes clack, clack. Back and forth. Back and forth. How many of these exchanges have I been in? And they're all the same. Like I'm reliving them again and again, only changing the lighting and the costumes. Is this one any different? Maybe it is. Maybe I just can't remember anymore.

"That's right, no one has," she says. "I wonder where he went."

"Maybe he just moved away without telling anyone."

"I'm looking for a man named Joe Neminis. Think you can find where *he* went?"

Lance: when you don't know the song, pretend you do.

"Everyone's looking for someone … something," I say and turn my attention to the ceiling.

She doesn't like being ignored. She wants all eyes on her. All the time. And although I'm not looking at her, she has my complete attention. Find Joe Neminis. There was a time when that's all I thought about. I figured it was the right thing to do, to find Mr. Neminis. I believed he killed my brothers. I believed he killed my father. I used to believe in a lot of things; now I believe in two: money and Scotch. I knew there would be no vengeance. I knew my brothers and my father weren't coming back. I gave up the hunt for Joe Neminis.

"Describe him," I say.

Something interesting: Her description of Joe Neminis is a bundle of contradictions, making it seem like she doesn't actually want me to find him. Except, I've seen him before, and if someone asked me, I'd describe him the same way. A pulsing, glowing paradox. No one talking about Neminis sounds like themselves. Everyone has intense reactions.

"He's a good man," she says. "A really good man."

"What? Was under the impression there weren't ..."

"Joe's the last."

"Why you so worried about him?"

"I just am. He was good to me; now I'm returning the favor."

"Do unto others ..."

"Something like that. When I find him, I'll be free." Then, she says, "By the way, are you going to tell me your first name? Everyone just calls you Lincoln."

"So should you. My first name's Abraham."

"Really?" This time she openly laughs. They all laugh. "Nice helmet," she says as she gets up.

"It's a trophy from the FOP."

"It's all rusty."

"Huh," I say.

I grab a drink and immediately get the impression that I've been duped, tricked, imprisoned. When she's gone, one of the balls on the desk gadget falls off, like a drumbeat that's a bit late.

Lincoln and the Sign
Of the sign located without of Lincoln's office, and of its importance.

The Missionary, looking down at you, his fervor gone, replaced by pity, will take his hat off, wipe his brow with a pocket handkerchief, and ask, "Son, are you all right?"

"Sure, never better," will be your reply as you curl into a fetal position on the gray-tiled floor at the feet of the Missionary.

"Hey, what's your name? What do your friends call you?"

"Friends …"

"Sure."

"Name's Lincoln. Says so on the sign," you'll say, pointing in no particular direction.

"Sign? What sign? Aren't any signs anywhere," the Missionary will say, looking out the door.

"Used to be. They were all over. You followed them. They led you places."

"What's your first name?"

You will remain quiet, hiding from the light, half-asleep on the floor.

"Son, I don't know. … You look awful … lost."

"Lost."

"Like a man who has lost his way."

"Can't blame me."

"Oh?"

"There aren't any signs."

"If there were a sign with your name on it, what would the first name be?"

Pause.

"Abraham."

The Missionary will not laugh.

Lincoln and the Showdown

How Epi Agravan and Morty Seneca disclosed the affair between Lance Malfet and Gwen Armathie, and how Agravan and Seneca disclosed the affair between Ambrose Armathie and Le Fey, and how Lance Malfet and Ambrose Armathie did battle.

A NAME YOU CAN TRUST

The police station. Just before the riots began. Desks overturned. Papers scattered. Officers and detectives everywhere. All with their mouths open. Their eyes wide. In the midst of their own battles. Cop against cop. But frozen. Stopped. To look. Mayor Ambrose Armathie lay on the floor. A puddle of thick, reddish liquid on the black and white tile next to him. Black and white hexagonal tile, blackandwhite hextile, blood. Lance Malfet hunched down. Head covered. An ivory-handled Colt SAA at his feet. Behind Malfet, two detectives. One with a lurid grin. The other stoic.

A hand reaches into the frame. A hand reaching toward the Colt.

Years of progress and prosperity, ruined. Lincoln was fighting Cirque Senechal when the shot was fired; Armathie had drawn his antique pistol; Malfet had taken it away from him; Armathie charged; the gun went off. The fight broke out between the chief of police and the mayor, between Malfet and Armathie, because the mayor learned the chief of police was sleeping with his wife, with Gwen Armathie, with *Mrs. Armathie*, and because the chief of police learned that Armathie was sleeping with a gangster, with Le Fey. Neither of them understood the irony of this battle. The narcissism. Epi Agravan and Morty Seneca, who believed they should be detectives and not beat cops, who believed they should be made detectives before *Lincoln*, who might have been in league with Le Fey, who *were* in league with Le Fey, decided to bring down the house of cards, decided to let chaos reign (or had it always reigned? Had it gone unnoticed?): one with a lurid grin, the other stoic.

In the picture: a feminine hand reaches toward the Colt.

Lincoln and the Jug
How Cirque Senechal made mockery of Lincoln, and how Morty Seneca spoke of a jug.

Morty Seneca lives on the outskirts of town in a house that is more a castle than a home. It has a natural moat in twin streams that run around the castle's island. You have to drive over a bridge to reach the complex. You have to be invited or expected for them to lower the bridge. I knew the place, once. It was owned by Joseph Armathie, a one-time mayor of Winchester and foster father to Lance Malfet. Later, Ambrose, Joseph's blood son, owned the castle when Ambrose became mayor. All three of them, Joseph, Ambrose, and Lance, had been the chief of police at one time or another. Now it's Morty Seneca's—a chief of everything the WPD used to fight. When there was a WPD. …

At the door I'm greeted by the butler, Cirque Senechal. An old friend. He's happy to see me.

"I'm *so* happy to see you. You must be the … detective," as if the word's acidic. I hope it burns through his tongue.

"How'd you guess?" I say.

Cirque used to be a desk cop. He likes to pretend he doesn't know me. He predicted I wouldn't make a good detective. And yet, here I am, and there he is.

"Oh, the scent of cheap booze and the evident lack of familiarity with a razor."

"You must be the … butler," I say.

"How *did* you guess?"

"Oh, the scent of arrogance and the evident lack of anything to back it up."

"Touché."

When Cirque turns his back to lead me inside, I take a hit from my flask. We walk down a marble hall that a legion of knights in full armor could've marched through. Tapestries hang everywhere. One of the tapestries shows a tree that depicts hanged men for leaves. There's a woman at the bottom of the tree smiling. I think I dated her once. I got confused when she said she liked hanged men.

Luckily, Cirque silently leads the way through the house, never looking at me, so I can continue drinking in peace. Keeps the memories away. Keeps the unwanted songs from playing.

Maybe it's the alcohol, but I get the unnerving feeling that none of this is actually happening; I feel like I'm walking through a haze of memories jerry-rigged together into a nightmare that I can't escape, a nightmare where I'm searching and searching for something, for an answer, but I only come up with more questions. Gotta be the alcohol.

Outside, Morty Seneca, wearing a white suit, sits next to a swimming pool.

"Mr. Lincoln, nice to see you. I'm a man who likes to get down to business. Cirque tells me you're looking for Joe Neminis," Seneca says. He's average height and build, has a dark tint to his skin. Italian or Greek. His hair is black and short, and he has a thin, black mustache. He wears mirrored sunglasses to show people how insignificant they are compared to him. His expression never changes. The digits in his Swiss bank account never stop changing—always increasing. There was a time when I would've done anything to get this close to Seneca, to haul him in, book him, make sure he ended up in prison. Now, I work for money.

"Yeah, I was wondering if you could give me any information about where he might be," I say.

"Ahh, where is anyone, for that matter? Some are here. Some are there. But even when you find them, you haven't really found them," he says in a deadpan.

"What?"

"Everyone is so agitated. Why don't they calm down? Take things as they come. There's no changing the world. So, sit back. Watch. And when it's your time to go, go," which is easy to say when you have a castle and your own smarmy butler.

But I figure Seneca's playing some angle. So, I play mine: ninety degrees … do unto others. … "Look. I was hired by Morgan Aurum to look for …"

"Mr. Neminis is what he was meant to be, just as you are who you were meant to be. So, feel free to drink from your flask."

Maybe on some other day I would've been embarrassed that he saw me drinking behind Cirque on the way in. Not today. Like Lance used to say: when life gives you lemons, make whisky sours.

"Do you know where Joe Neminis is?" I ask.

"I'm sure he'll surface again," says Seneca.

"And what if he doesn't?"

"Ah, well. That's the way it goes."

"You don't sound too concerned."

"That's because I care about him as much as I care about a jug."

"A jug?"

"A jug." He pauses. "You see, Mr. Lincoln, there are powers at work that we don't understand, that have planned out everything for us. By questioning, we disrespect those powers. By becoming concerned, we offend those powers. Capiche?"

Listening to this babble, I get the unnerving feeling that I'm in a room all by myself, with the walls closing in, that I've been trapped here by some murderous madman with a riddle for me to solve. But I don't know the answer.

"I'm sorry, I seem to have forgotten. What language are we speaking again?"

"Mr. Lincoln, can't you see? It's all right in front of you."

"I don't follow, Mr. Seneca."

"I know, Mr. Lincoln. Most people don't follow. Or, actually, most people do follow but think they're leading."

"What are you doing, Mr. Seneca: leading or following?"

He doesn't answer.

"Hmm, what would Le Fey think?" I say.

Seneca remains stoic.

The only interesting piece of information he gives me is this: Seneca used to be married to Morgan. Or thought he was. His mistake. Morgan actually married half his money. And after six months, she took her love, the money, on a honeymoon never to return.

"Weren't you angry?" I ask, testing him.

"No, Mr. Lincoln."

"A jug, huh?"

"A jug."

LINCOLN AND THE PROPHECY

Of the vision that Lincoln saw, and how his vision was expounded.

The usual hangover depression filling your body, replacing the euphoria of your stupor, a headache will come throbbing, feeling like two generators were implanted into your temples, and they will build in intensity, set to fire electrical charges between them like a cerebral Jacob's Ladder, giving you the unnerving sensation that you are about to receive an interstellar, perhaps interplanar, transmission: a prophecy. You will then no longer think your own thoughts.

"Maybe it'd be better that way," you'll say.

"What? Better what way?" from the Missionary.

But you won't reply.

"You know, Lincoln, if you put your faith in ..." The Missionary will trail off, start again, trail off again, stop completely, shake his head, toss his Bible into the corner. It will fall open to Psalms, but no one will feel like singing. "Why'd you start drinking, Lincoln?"

"Looking for something I lost."

"What did you lose?"

"Something I didn't know I had."

"How'd you know it was gone?"

The electricity will pulse stronger and stronger until you can almost ..., and then you will see the blue lightning, coalescing into a chapel, the windows broken out, the altar desecrated, light from fires burning in the distance reflecting off the shards on the ground, and here there are two chairs, and one chair is wormeaten, rotten, and the other chair is fully intact and holds a plant from which sprouts flowers, flowers growing out of previous flowers and copious amounts of fruit (but what kind?) growing from the last flower, and perched on the chairs are two birds, one wonderfully white, one wonderfully black, and you will realize that this is the transmission, that this is the prophecy, but that only churls and priests can interpret prophecies, so you will turn to your own churl, the Missionary, and ask, in a burned-out voice, the voice of one who sees:

"Hey, padre ... what's it all about?"

And he will look at you and say, "I have no idea."

LINCOLN AND THE SHIELD
How Joseph Armathie likened the Shield to the world, and how the manifold offices and awards should be conferred.

The Fraternal Order of Police badge is round. Silver. The letters FOP are in blue. It was called the shield. In the background, an enlarged version. In the foreground, Joseph Armathie. Former mayor Joseph Armathie. Smiling. Hands held in the air, standing at the foot of a podium. His son, Ambrose Armathie, atop the podium. Announcing Lance Malfet, the next chief of police. Announcing partners Lincoln and Bors, detectives of the year. Then the junior Armathie's acceptance speech. He shook Lincoln's hand. And Bors'. He hugged Malfet. The senior Armathie made a speech. He explained the shield; it was round because the world was round, and that is what police officers gave up to be police officers. The world. It should be no surprise that cops have trouble in the real world, then. Because they do not live in it. But it cannot go on without them.

LINCOLN AND THE CONUNDRUM
Of the riddle of Epi Agravan, and how Lincoln bethought him of the quest at large.

The next name on my list is Epi Agravan. He lives outside of town, too: Camelot Estates. It's a gated community designed to keep the undesirables out and the uninviting in. Epi's a dealer of drugs and illegal porn and a pimp. Sometimes I feel bad for Epi. If only there were more sordid enterprises to be involved in. Reality has always held this poor guy back.

So far, I have nothing. No leads. No tips. Not even sure there's a case, that there's a Morgan Aurum, that "Joe Neminis" isn't some codeword I've been fed and duped into passing around, that, at the end of it all, I'll be the successful private detective who gives the logical explanation describing the entire affair and then all the bad guys will go to jail—maybe I'll end up the expendable messenger.

I take another swig from my flask, which I filled at Seneca's bar. The air outside Agravan's is full of raucous, horrible music and feedback. I can't imagine what he could add to this case.

I knock on the door. The house is your average upper-middle-class house: partially brick, partially vinyl siding, big windows, roof with too many points, none of them final.

"Hey, come on in, my man," says Agravan.

He enunciates each word as if he's consciously trying to keep them in order. He's a short, fat, drunken man with a bald head. Not completely bald—he has that annoying ring of hair that wraps around from the temples to the back. He wears sunglasses with red lenses and silver, wire frames. Poor sap, no one told him he isn't twenty anymore. He shows me inside. Luckily, he shuts the stereo off.

Like Lance always told me: After a while of doing this job, you get to thinking that you've never actually left your office, that everything actually takes place there, that you only imagine different decorations or levels of glamour or seediness for entertainment purposes. And when it's all over, where do you end up? Sitting there

A NAME YOU CAN TRUST

by yourself, itching to find a reason so you can imagine it all again. Only slightly different this time. Maybe with crazier names for the characters. Maybe in a different city for a change of pace.

Agravan's place looks like a frat house: four mismatched couches, posters of women in (but also mostly out of) bikinis, stolen street signs, a mammoth television that's either on the fritz or broadcasting Epi's glitching stream of consciousness. The floor is stained with spilled beer, covered with black circles where cigarettes and joints have been squashed out because the only ashtray is overflowing. There're about two kilos of coke on the coffee table. A sign on the wall says:

I Have Never Made a Mistake in My Life.
I Thought I Did One Time,
but I Was Mistaken.

Underneath this sign are three headlines stapled to the wall: "Seneca Exonerated" and "Mayor Armathie Shot" and "Agravan Acquitted." Take things as they come. There's no changing the world. The powers that be have it all planned out.

"So, my man, *what is up?*" asks Agravan, chugging a Schlitz.

"Are you asking for a definition?" I say, hitting my flask.

He smiles; beer runs down his chin. "Hey, my man, is this about Lanny?"

"Who?"

"Lanny Malfet. You know, that guy, man, who, far out?, dig it?, like, uh, yeah! It's just so fucked up. Shit-shit-shit, can hardly believe it myself," says Agravan.

"You mind running that by me again?"

"It's just a pity, man."

"What?"

"*It*. You know? The thing, man."

"Look, I was wondering if you had any information on …"

"Now you're, you know, fuck, pullin' this five-O, like, detective shit on me, my man. Come on. Eat, drink, and be, you know, right?, know what I'm sayin' here? Be happy 'cause tomorrow … Wow, I tell ya: fucked up. Fucked up, man." He nods gravely, pops another Schlitz, shotguns it.

I take a long hit from my flask. There is no case. There is no point. There is no conductor. The music is discordant. I should just lay my head in that cocaine. It'd save a hitman the trouble.

"Hey, uh, you know where Joe Neminis is?" I ask, casually.

"Saw him the other day. Who wants to know?"

"I do. Didn't you just hear me, or were you out somewhere?"

"Far out, bro."

"Don't reel yourself in on my account."

"Uh, yeah. Cool. He finally came over. Hadn't, you know, um, seen him since, fuckin' A, since the old days. Good drinkin' buddy, Joe. You know what I'm saying?"

"You slur a lot, but I get the idea. So, when did you see him?"

"Hoo! Man, when the hell, it had to've been yesterday. …"

"Yesterday?"

"Or maybe, man, like, you know?, last month. Maybe. Shit, bro, I can't remember. Uh, you talked to Morty?"

"Yeah."

"Joe wasn't there?"

"No."

"Huh. Good old Joe." Agravan goes to drink his Schlitz but finds it's empty. He looks at my flask.

I mumble, "This is going nowhere," and hand him the flask. Like Lance always said … screw it. …

"Can't you see, man?" Agravan asks.

"What?"

"It's, like, you know?, all right in front of you. And you're, fuck, trying to, uh, put your P. I. mojo on it, but, hell. You know what I'm sayin'?"

"Someone ought to."

"Joe Neminis. Lanny. You. Me. Morty. It's all a puzzle. A riddle. A *conundrum.*"

"A conundrum? Where'd you hear that word?"

"You don't wanna know, buddy. Wooh! You *don't* wanna know."

He was right. I didn't.

Lincoln and the Visions
Of an advision which the Missionary had, and how he fought and overcame his adversary.

When the vision is gone, when there is only the afterglow of the electricity, you will be on the floor trying to figure out why you're on the floor trying to stop the pulsing in your head. But it won't stop. And your new friend won't stop talking. And you won't know who your new friend is. Still.

"Before I was a …" he'll look at the Bible, "I was a junkie. My wife, too. Then, one day, I thought God sent me a vision through a pink laser off a girl's necklace. I was sleeping in a room when a sentient spear attacked me. I figured that was the heroin. Once I was finally able to break the spear, I was attacked by a knight —and I couldn't see his face. I thought that was addiction. After a hard-fought battle, I finally defeated the knight. But then, I was attacked by a lion and a dragon with golden letters burned into his forehead. The lion, I figured, was the law because I took it down without a problem. I wasn't a dealer; I was an addict. So, the law might look fierce, but once I was ready to give up my habit, it would pad away like a housecat. The dragon, though, was a different matter. I didn't know what the dragon stood for. All I knew was that I wanted to destroy him, but I also wanted to read the golden letters that were burned into his forehead. Each time I got close, the dragon would attack, I'd dodge, and then I wasn't able to see the letters. Strangely, in this battle, there was a leopard helping me (who I figured symbolized my wife). But I didn't want the leopard to beat the dragon for me because then I wouldn't get to read the golden message. I wouldn't learn what I was supposed to learn. Since it was taking me so long to fight the dragon, though, I was getting tired. Until I finally collapsed. Still, I kept trying to read the message on the dragon's forehead, the golden message, if only I could see it. But I never could. Finally, after a long fight with the leopard, the dragon exploded into a cloud of little dragons. And although I felt myself being freed from something, I was, at the same time, terrified by this confusion of wyverns.

"As soon as I snapped to, I took my wife and went to the methadone clinic. I never figured out what the message on the dragon's head was, so I decided it said ..." He'll look at the Bible again. "Later on, I had another vision. Maybe it was a dream. Maybe just a memory.

There were two chairs: one rotten, one good; there were two birds: one black, one white. It was all in a rundown chapel. But I didn't know what it meant," he'll say.

You'll say: "Well, you're a regular good guy. ..." and trail off, staring into your friend's eyes, looking for golden letters there that will give you the answer, hoping for, thinking you see ... but you'll know there aren't any letters. You'll only wish there were.

LINCOLN AND THE CELEBRATION
A wonderful tale of the feast for Lincoln.

Lincoln sits in a room by himself. Party favors are scattered on the floor, along with a couple revelers. Sleeping. A single poker room light from the ceiling. Lincoln sits in a room. By himself. Before there was Joseph Armathie, Ambrose Armathie, Lance Malfet, Cirque Senechal, Mortimer Seneca, Epi Agravan. Lincoln had just made detective. The Armathies and Malfet, who had made the decision, were very happy for Lincoln. Senechal, Seneca, Agravan, they disapproved. Through the entire party, amongst all of the cops, Lincoln could always hear Senechal, Seneca, Agravan, whispering. Whispering. He didn't know about what, except when they disdainfully mentioned him. He also heard them mention Le Fey; he heard them mention Mrs. Armathie, but he didn't think anything of it. Soon the three dissenters left. Most stayed. Throughout the entire party, Joseph smiled (he smiled a lot), drank Scotch, talked to everyone. Slowly people left. Then Joseph left. Ambrose passed out on the floor. Lincoln turned to talk to

Malfet, but, as often happens at parties, Malfet had disappeared. So, Lincoln sat in a room. By himself. The party was over. There were only the pictures.

LINCOLN AND THE JOYOUS ISLE
Of Dr. Turkwin, and how Lincoln came into the Joyous Isle, and of other matters.

The last thing Agravan told me was that he used to date Morgan, back when he was younger, better looking. Probably she was cheating on Seneca with him. When he started getting fat, when his hair fell out, she took off. Wanted nothing to do with him. Not a word or a note. Much like Seneca, though, he didn't do anything about it. He kept on living his life. I suppose Seneca and Agravan were happy to have had her for a little while. No matter how bad she treated them. But what doesn't make sense is, what's a woman like Morgan Aurum doing chasing after anyone? It reminds me of that tree with all the hanged men for leaves. ... Why does she want to find Joe Neminis? Is there a leaf missing? Whose side am I on? Hers or my own? Morgan shouldn't ever have to look for anything. She *always* gets what she wants. So, if she's searching, maybe I don't want to find what she's looking for. ...

It's time for the last name on the list: J. P. Kamis. He's bound to be interesting due to his residence: Joyous Isle Mental Hospital. It's one of those Gothic buildings that couldn't possibly be anything other than an insane asylum or a prison.

Dr. Turkwin meets me at the desk. "Mr. Lincoln, I presume," says Dr. Turkwin. He's bald, thin, wears dark-blue sunglasses.

"What's with the shades, doctor?" I say.

"The eyes are the portal to the soul. And you don't want those who are mad to gaze into your soul, now do you?" he answers as if this were obvious.

"I don't want to tell you how to do your job, doctor …"

"Here it comes anyway."

"… but don't you have to develop a relationship with your patients?"

"My patients are the severely deranged. Even evil. We share nothing in common. I am above them, have risen above them because of my superior intellect, because of my powerful mind. What they think of me doesn't matter." His eyebrows arch above his shades.

"You're the doctor, doctor." Though if your psychiatrist is diagnosing people as *evil*, maybe you need a new psychiatrist.

"Indeed. What is this all about, anyway?"

"I'm looking for Joe Neminis."

"Sounds like a social disease. So, what will you have when you find him?"

I follow Dr. Turkwin down poorly lit halls with leaking ceilings, by rooms filled with the past and future valedictorians of this Laughing Academy (though the only person here who should be locked up is the shrink), until we come to Mr. Kamis' room. Dr. Turkwin turns to me.

"Be very careful with this one. He is—what do the plebeians say?—playing with a few fiddles short of an orchestra. He has a way of pretending to be perfectly sane, and just when you think you can trust him, he attacks. Physically. He is in a straitjacket, but he has escaped before."

"I think I can take care of myself."

He lets me inside. The room is square, with padded walls (of course). It smells of urine and shit, and the only light comes in through a barred window about fifteen feet up. J. P. faces the corner, away from the light.

"Mr. Kamis, I need to ask you a few questions about Joe Neminis."

"Questions? Why ask questions?"

"To get answers," I reply. "To reconstruct the past and possibly predict the future."

"But there are no answers, the past is frozen and unattainable; the future is only a probability."

"To get meaning. I'm trying to find the meaning of Joe's disappearance."

"How can there be meaning? Do you think life's a newspaper puzzle?"

I'm getting a headache. I want my flask. This is tedious. Eat, drink, and … "To tell you the truth, I have no idea."

"Nobody knows anything because there's nothing to know. There are only experiences. Experiences in the present. … What are you really doing here?" Kamis says, still facing the corner.

"I just told you. I've been sent by Morgan Aurum to find Joe Neminis. …"

"*Who?!*" screams Kamis, and as I see him leaping through the air, I realize there isn't enough money in the world for me to complete this case.

On the ground, Kamis and I are in a struggle for who knows what reason. My mind is removed from the entire ordeal. As if it's not happening to me. As if I don't care about the outcome. As if I'm so hepped up on dope, I can't recognize the world for a fantasy anymore. As if I now understand why Ms. Aurum's looking for Neminis, as if I understand the entire case, and I don't want to be a part of it. The money's not that important. But everything that I couldn't see ... it was all right there ... and suddenly Kamis' face is familiar. As if I've known him my whole life. And that fact breaks me of the anger and rage ... okay, the apathetic greed and petty vengeance that have ruled my brain since the day Ambrose Armathie went into a coma, the day two of my brothers and my father died in the ensuing Winchester Riots, the day I got so drunk I wanted to attack the first person I met, but since I was sloshed, the first person I met made short work of me, and a homeless woman told me my assailant's name (or probably made up a name), the day the harmony of the music ceased and became a discordant roar. The day the conductor stepped out, perhaps never to return. Perhaps never there in the first place.

Finally, both of us bloodied and bruised, my sparring partner asks me my name. He asks who sent me. He asks why I was sent. He says I have to answer because I'm the first one who fought him to a draw. He says I have to tell him the truth, this time.

"I'm looking for Joe Neminis. I think I ran into him once, and I had it in my mind to ... I was sent by Morgan Aurum, who I now know is Morgan Le Fey." Then I say: "My name's Lincoln."

He says: "Perceval." He says: "Joe Neminis is what ..."

Then Kamis collapses. Soon after, I feel a sharp pain in my neck. I mumble, "Lance," for that's who Kamis is. The room goes fuzzy.

When I wake up, I'm in my own cell in the Laughing Academy. I look over at the door, and there's Dr. Turkwin. I figure he thinks I'm head of my class.

"How are you feeling today?" he asks.

"Like five-thousand bucks. You can't keep me in here forever, you know."

"But you have been here forever already, Mr. Neminis."

"I'm not Joe Neminis, doc."

"Of course you're not, Mr. Lincoln. But we can pretend. It's fun to pretend."

LINCOLN AND FAITH
How the Missionary came to beg Lincoln his name, and of other matters marvelous.

The headache will begin to subside. You will stand up and walk to your desk, grab the bottle of whisky.

The Missionary will say, "You know, I've heard that, looking through a telescope, you see the past, present, and the future."

"Oh yeah?"

"Yeah. The stars are the past. The planets, comets, meteors are the present. The darkness is the future. But if we could pinpoint our places in that darkness, then we'd always know where to go."

"The problem is, it's darkness," you'll say. "And there isn't any conductor to direct us through it."

"You're right. So how about this: I think we should team up."

"To do what?" you'll say.

"Search."

"What'll we search for?"

"That which was lost. In the darkness."

"Sure, I'll drink to that."

"Only, you're gonna have to tell me your real name."
"No problem. But you can't laugh."
"I won't."
"How do you know you won't?"
"Because I have ... because I ... I just won't."
"Good. But tell me something."
"Sure."

"Do you think orchestras actually need a conductor, or is the conductor just some madman waving his arms around at the front?"

LINCOLN AND THE CAUSE
How Lincoln delivered Tristram out of prison, and how Lincoln was made detective, and how a dumb maid spake, and brought him to the Shield.

Far in the distance, a man exits the gates of a prison. He is seen from behind. He wears a new gray suit, black shoes, and even a fedora. The sun is breaking through the clouds. Or is being covered up by them. There is nothing else in the picture, except the man, the gates, the squat guardhouse, the sandy ground, the sky.

The man's name was Mr. Tristram. He had been imprisoned accidentally. And Lincoln had freed him. When everyone else thought Mr. Tristram was guilty, when everyone thought Mr. Tristram was a murderer, Lincoln, Officer (not yet detective) Lincoln believed him. Believed Tristram when he claimed innocence. So, Lincoln put in extra hours, hours without pay, dangerous hours, hours where he could've lost his job if he'd been caught. And Lincoln found the evidence. The evidence that set Mr. Tristram free. The accused is no one of import. Lincoln didn't know him before the case, and Lincoln never saw him again afterward.

Following the case, a quiet filing clerk, a reticent filing clerk, beloved by Joseph Armathie, well, she praised Lincoln. For going above and beyond the call. For fighting against paranoia, blind vengeance, knee-jerk reactions, she spoke in favor of Lincoln to the point where Joseph and Ambrose Armathie, and Lance Malfet decided to make Lincoln a detective. Some sneered. Mr. Tristram went free.

The sun broke through the clouds.

LINCOLN AND THE FUTURE
Of the great danger which Lincoln was in, and how he saw a serpent and a lion fight, and of other bizarre matters.

I sit on the floor of the Joyous Isle Mental Hospital. They've done a great job. They even have my square of Polaroids arranged on the wall. With all the drugs coursing through my veins, though, I can't think so well. I have no idea how long I've been in here.

I get a visitor. How nice. It's Morgan. She makes out with Dr. Turkwin. Then she comes in.

"So, what did you find out? Do you know where he is?" she asks.

"Yep," I bluff.

"Well …"

I stare at the ceiling.

"Well, where is he?" She grabs my chin and looks into my eyes. Without her sunglasses, maybe she could've stared me down.

"Ah, where is anyone for that matter? Some are here. Some are there. You know, man?" I give an awkward laugh. It seems like someone else's.

"What?!"

"There is no Joe Neminis. But then, of course there is."

Morgan jabs me with a long fingernail. "You better start making sense. I know what you're on, and you shouldn't be this high. So, give me the story."

"Ah, you want the logical explanation from the private detective."

"Whatever."

"Okay: you're married to Seneca, and you took his money; you're with Agravan, and you took his youth; you're with Malfet … oh, I mean Kamis, and you took his sanity; you're with Ambrose, and you almost took his life; but you can't find Joe Neminis, so you can't take his …"

She looks at me from behind those sunglasses. I wish I could take them off, see what she's thinking. But then, what would I know?

"You're quite amazing, Le Fey," I say. "A regular sorceress."

In my mind I think of a lion fighting a snake, and you'd think a lion would have the edge on the snake, but snakes are quick, they have fangs, venom, and in the end, really, the smart money's on the snake because the lion is big and proud and regal, but no one ever had a lion sneak up on him in the night, no one was ever tricked by a lion, and then I think of going to Armathie's castle during the height of the riots, and the speakers to his stereo blared with feedback, and I walked from room to room, amazed at the damage, as if my entire world had been destroyed, as if the capital of the world had been leveled, and after seeing it all, I broke down in the chapel, where I saw two birds, one white, one black; I saw two chairs, one rotten with worms, one holding a bizarre plant with flowers inside of flowers inside of flowers but then finally holding fruit, and on the ground I saw my partner, Bors, who I thought was dead because he was strung out on the floor, and I felt like it all meant something—I wanted it to mean something; I wanted to be able to take this symbol and make it define my existence. But now, I see the chapel as just another room that needs refurbishing. Only this time, it should be an observatory.

Morgan's arm goes around her back and returns to her side. She holds a Colt SAA. Ivory-handled.

"Where is Joe Neminis?" she says, placing the barrel of the gun on my forehead.

Where are you, Lincoln? Figure it out. What *is* happening? Morgan Le Fey, playing the part she was trained to play, has lured you to an insane asylum hoping to scare you enough to give her the information. But as you sit here, as Morgan waits, Lance Malfet is freeing himself from his cell, is setting the rest of the missing cops free, is taking Dr. Turkwin down, is opening the door to your very own cell, Lincoln, is wresting you free of Le Fey, is (as expected) disappearing—again. So, you can stop thinking about Morgan. The Colt will not be fired. Morgan Le Fey will not kill you. She's not even here. You might as well be back at your office, smoking a Pall Mall, drinking some Scotch. But what might happen to you, Lincoln? In the time to come? You have no explanation for the past. No tight, easy monologue. No distanced clarification of the facts. The present is too chaotic. So, the bad guys will not go to prison. Not now, anyway. But you will not be the disposable messenger. You will have to face the music of the morrow. There will be no simple way to define your future. Yet you will try.

Perhaps *this* is what will happen.

LINCOLN AND THE HOLY GRAIL
How each of them knew other, and of their great courtesy, and how, by miracle, they were both made whole by the coming of the holy vessel of Sangreal.

"Padre, my name's Abraham Lincoln," you'll say.

The Missionary will slink down.

"Seriously. But most of my life, I went by my middle name: Perceval."

"Perceval Lincoln?" The Missionary will be markedly surprised. "Perceval. It's me. I can't believe ... You look so different. But it's me: I'm Diogenes Bors. Don't you recognize me? Am I that changed?"

After a while, through years of haze, the both of you will remember each other.

You'll say, "Gene ... I ... uhhh ..."

"Sung like a prodigy."

Then Bors will mention the fact that you'll need money to fund your quest. Your quest for what was lost. And you'll reach into your pocket and pull out a five-thousand-dollar bill.

"I'm sure this portrait of Madison will help us some," you'll say.

"Where'd you get that, Lincoln?"

"There isn't enough Scotch in the world for that story."

You will walk through the doorway, still holding the whisky bottle, which, once outside, you will heave in the direction of the sun, the bottle spinning, spinning, until it is in direct proximity to that burning orb that blots out the darkness, leaving you with the present and the past, and you will hope that it'll turn into, that Sol with the power of the heavens will transform it into a glittering beacon, a symbol, a cup, a chalice, the Holy Grail. But you will remember about the signs, about the golden letters, about the chairs and the plant in the chapel, and know that it'll merely remain a whisky bottle that's about to smash into the ground. Somehow that will be comforting. And then the both of you, Perceval and Bors, will set out in search of Lance Malfet and Joe Neminis; you will move forth on a day, perhaps a Friday, perhaps any other day, for the sake of humankind. Perhaps.

IDENTITY THEFT

While you read this, your identity is being stolen, has been stolen. Before you were confident in who you were: you were yourself; before you were confident in who others were: they were themselves. You could not be them; they could not be you. Or so you thought until now when, you find, someone has broken the rules. He no longer wished to be himself, she no longer wished to be herself, they no longer wished to be themselves; instead, the person in question, in order to cast aside their true identity, has decided to become you. The you who is not you. And whether or not the new you acts in a way that you would act, really doesn't matter. Because now *they are you*.

Although the choice to become you may have been relatively random, the plan that led to it was not. Cognizant or no, it turns out that you are very good with computers, that you hacked into various websites containing bank account and credit card and Social

Security numbers, that you were able to forge signatures, speak in different voices, even becoming a master of disguise in order to create accounts you would later close; furthermore, you opened several new credit cards in your own name that you operated with the help of a league of associates you've never met in order to establish an excellent rating, to replace that entry-level plastic with gold and then platinum, all for the purpose of establishing the new you, the you who is not you.

Once you were substantiated, the you who is not you hit the road. The escapade began small but along the way continued to snowball until it consisted of a troupe of heterogeneous hooligans chauffeured by a legion of Hummer limos, a debaucherous odyssey spanning the entire country, paid for by the touchless tapping of the cards, augmented by cash advances when the products or services desired were owned or enacted by those who prefer (and probably require) the anonymity of green. Along the way you drank drinks you wouldn't drink at bars you can't imagine going to, ate food you wouldn't eat if threatened at restaurants you've never even heard of, took drugs you wouldn't take administered to you by underworld types you figured only existed in movies, consorted with sex workers you wouldn't even so much as touch (well, okay, maybe once, just to see what it's like), agreed to wagers whose odds dictate that no one in their right mind would ... but you did, made friends with people of a dubious nature who couldn't possibly be real—none of whom you remember anyhow, and, in general, had adventures of the sort found only in tabloid descriptions of celebrity benders, old timey *Penthouse Letters* that begin with "I never thought that this would happen to me," and the more outrageous pieces of journalism by Dr. Hunter S. Thompson (now deceased), and perhaps the worst part, for how much it's costing you, the real you, you don't even know about any of it.

When you finally learn of the jag you've been on, you will suffer an identity crisis. In trying to explain to various customer-service representatives that you've never opened a credit card with their particular bank, that as a general rule you never take cash advances because the interest rates are outrageous, that you've never been to Jean-Georges, or, for that matter, Tijuana, that it's unlikely you and everyone you know could consume enough alcohol to equal a thousand-dollar bar tab really anywhere, that you seriously doubt the listed massage specialists graduated from an accredited school of massotherapy, so why would you go there, your complaints will fall on deaf ears, for all of the call-center operators will inform you that you are not who you claim to be. The real you can be found in your credit evaluation, can be found in the paper trail strewn across now three countries. And it continues still.

But what will keep you going as you make endless telephone calls, as you press countless numbers to reach real human beings who may not exist, as you wait for the next representative who may be illusory, as you hear those dreaded words: "Do you mind if I put you on hold," knowing full well that they spell certain doom, as you are (unsurprisingly) disconnected, as you resignedly try the call again again again, yes, through all of this, what *will* keep you going? Beauty. The promise of beauty will help you persevere. The beauty of that sought-after moment when you smile, or perhaps sigh a contented sigh. The beauty of honestly and truthfully saying to the last customer-service representative, "No-no, thank you." The beauty of hearing the line go dead. The beauty of setting the phone down and knowing that you do not have to pick it back up. The beauty of realizing that all of your actions from this point forth really will be *your* actions. The beauty of no longer being fused to the you who is not you. The beauty of being you all by yourself once again.

OUBLIETTE

Last night, in your town, a businessman stepped out of a sleek skyscraper, stretched, gazed at the darkening sky. You may remember that there were no stars, yet the moon shone brightly, as if the world were covered by a warm, comfortable haze through which a pleasant spotlight was gleaming. It was the type of evening imbued with the spirit of adventure, transforming even the most diehard morning person into a nocturnal animal seeking not contemplation nor rumination, but action. The warmth lent serenity; the spotlight goaded people on, casually urging that it was their time.

The businessman, having stretched and imbibed the alluring atmosphere, decided not to go directly home, decided, instead, to walk about town. If you were astir, and you might have been, you perhaps noticed the businessman making this decision, identifying the look of someone who has come upon an ostensibly momentous resolution.

Having settled his mind on the walk, the businessman turned to the main street and commenced. As you could see, as anyone could see, he was a confident man who knew his business. His stride evinced a readiness for anything, any adventure, any challenge. The moon shone on the businessman as if it were his own personal spotlight; hence, any action would hold the utmost importance, any situation would be handled with the utmost acumen.

Unsurprisingly to you, but a startling revelation to an infrequent perambulator in your town, the businessman stumbled upon a mendicant at the corner of a decaying brick building along the main street. As you are well aware, the vagrant is a mainstay; and, although no one knows his actual name, he is called by a sobriquet stemming from his affliction (so diagnosed by the many, many amateur psychologists who are your neighbors): Fuck You Bob (his affliction supposedly being Tourette's Syndrome). Bob lives at the corner of the dilapidated brick building, but he could live anywhere else. For he is also blind.

Upon conquering his astonishment, having been ignorant of the homeless problem in your town, the businessman looked at Bob with curiosity, still filled with the vigor of the night air; Bob replied with a string of epithets (but nothing else is to be expected), then smiled at the businessman. The businessman, who could certainly see that Bob was blind, was enthralled by the gesture. Walking by during this encounter (for you were there, let's not belabor the point any longer), you noticed that the two were staring at each other as if they were not sure the other existed (indeed, Bob had a partial excuse, although he had been struck). The businessman gaped at the wretch as if Bob were a visionary churl from an Arthurian tale, the entire scene lit by the spotlight moon, gleaming warmly from behind the haze.

If you were perspicacious, and you might have been (for who is to say but yourself?), perchance you noticed that the men were not merely staring at each other; they were enmeshed in a silent exchange. Neither one moved; Bob, as expected, would occasionally explode into a torrent of profanities (but nothing else is to be expected); no other physical actions were manifest. The conversation was only identifiable in the eyes of the interlocutors, for they were animated, darting, never resting in the other's gaze for too long, as if communicating through a form foreign to humankind.

You stopped to watch this oneiric colloquy. What could it mean? A night like last is full of possible meanings, the very landscape, the very sky, the very ground you walk on bursts with secret messages refusing to explain themselves. The invigorating power of the warm evening air coupled with the moon irradiates all with a fascinating brilliance, and you believe that if you were able to wrap your mind around each symbol, you would understand the whole of being. For instance, in this circumstance, there were two men staring at each other, and if not for their eyes, they could have been mannequins. Unlike most, you saw their eyes; and, combined with the galvanizing charge of the night, you wished to comprehend the significance of this esoteric tête-à-tête. Your heart beat faster until it was the only sound; you watched the two as if they were part of an augur's vision made flesh; you blocked out the world, hoping to catch a clue.

And then it was over. The businessman broke away from Bob and continued on. Still, the businessman was filled with the promise of the evening, hoping that an amusing adventure would befall him before his journey was through; and, after stepping away from Bob, if you could have seen the businessman's face (but you still stared at the now-vacant stage, erstwhile scaffold of the enthralling scene), you would have recognized that peculiar mien manifest in one who suddenly forgets something of, perhaps, the utmost importance— a moment ago the thought was prevalent; a moment later, it never existed ... but it had to have existed, if it were only possible to wrap one's mind around it. ... At last, you turned and saw the businessman saunter away, unable to summon the strength to charge up to him, to demand the import of, to demand an explanation for what had just occurred.

Unable. Instead, you looked on as he headed up the main street and then turned into a side alley, away from the light of the moon.

What you did not see was what happened in the alley.

The businessman was ambling up the main street, which you know so well, when he came upon the narrow way. As most of the townspeople have done, you have passed the alley many times before, but you have never ventured therein. In your town, whenever anyone wants to indulge in the sordid, they find more salubrious methods to do so. The businessman, too, might have overlooked the offshoot, for although he was in an adventurous mood, he was not prepared to descend deep into the bowels of the town, save for the fact that he heard a noise—ever so faint, but the man detected it. A drop of water? A cry for help? He only knew it was a sound. For a night like last night, that was enough.

Gazing down the narrow way, the man was met with those conflicting emotions of one who wishes to explore and one who knows better than to walk down any dark alley that exposes itself. And the alley was certainly dark, the type of darkness that is not merely devoid of light but that absorbs all light.

This was not a warm haze covering the earth. This was a black hole. And when you saw the man enter the alley, you were met with the distinct sensation that he had disappeared from the face of the planet. That he had been swallowed up.

The alley was sweltering and smelled faintly of fish —a smell not completely unattractive. For it was not the smell of rotting fish, nor the smell of a fish market, but fish just the same.

Standing near the opening of the alley, the man called, "Hello," but no answer came. Until, again, he heard a faint sound identical to the one before. He followed the sound.

Walking deeper into the tenebrous alley, the man realized he was on a steep declivity. With each step downward, the darkness somehow grew thicker. It appeared that the inky blackness would never end, when, at that moment, the man came upon a light. Comparable to the moon, it was also far off, perhaps miles away, and the atmosphere being pitch, the luminescence more resembled an amber nightlight, rather than a theater's spot.

With the caliginous, fetid, sudorific atmosphere, the man was beginning to feel giddy. Stumbling along, at one point he quickly turned around to see that he could no longer locate the entrance to the alley; after spinning, the man could no longer be certain in which direction he was moving, for, although he saw a light, the light did not illuminate the way, it merely shone in spite of the darkness. Looking in each direction, the man saw, or perhaps imagined, myriad corridors bending off of the alley. But panic did not arise in the businessman. For he felt that this is what he always wanted: to be in the dark on an adventure unparalleled in his quotidian life. He groped through the blackness, inexperienced in such circumstances, to the point where the light ceased.

It was a hole in the ground. The hole was barely identifiable; without the light the businessman would have fallen into it—for he could certainly fit. The depth of the hole was unknown, for the light did not penetrate the darkness any farther than to unveil the hole, nor did the businessman lean over to inspect. He felt around, but that was all.

Again, the noise came. This time the businessman was able to pinpoint its emanation—whoever or whatever was moaning, was behind him. The noise was of little consequence any longer. The pleasant warmth of the inviting evening was now a stifling blare of heat. Sweat poured off the businessman's face into the cavity, as he finally bent over the top of it on his knees, arms around the borders.

He wanted to enter the hole. He wanted to dive down into the darkness. He wanted to seethe in the ubiquitous filth and blackness of this gully. He never wanted to be clean again. He wanted everything that his life was not, the polar opposite, the antipodes. He wanted to blot out all light. He wanted a world of chaos and stimulation. He wanted to descend into the underworld. He wanted to become the ruler of the underworld.

Yet, the businessman was split: one side yearned to descend, the other demanded to leave the alley immediately. The crux of the matter was how unassimilable the experience was. A businessman did not walk into unknown alleys; a businessman did not plunge into holes in unknown alleys. But that was why he wanted to do it. Afterward, he could walk amongst his fellow businesspersons, and they would never know that one of their own had crossed their antiseptic zone to the other side, had conquered the abyss.

The businessman rose, stalked around the hole, hoping to find an angle, hoping to ascertain what was inside. Such an angle did not exist. All his troubles gained him was another muffled moan—this one louder.

Crouching down, the man was about to submerge his head, when someone appeared. At first he could only hear breathing, then he saw the intruder's lips: they were heavily lipsticked and lined—a woman.

"Will you?" The woman's voice was emitted with the same whispering strain as the moan.

"What?" said the businessman.

"Now?"

"I don't know."

"What do you mean?"

"It's probably not a good idea."

"It's *your* business."

"I *know* what my business is."

The moan again, this time annoyed, more of a sigh. The man focused on the lips; they moved as entities unto themselves: two agents that proceeded in concert for some unknown, unknowable purpose. As unknowable, perhaps, as the symbols of the invigorating night.

"Why have you come here, then?"

"I was curious."

"Curious."

"It was this place—I'd never seen it before."

"This place …"

"I heard a noise."

"Shall I be quiet? I can be quiet."

"Yes. No."

"You *know* what you *want*. You want to find out."

"I …"

"It isn't that difficult."

"But I know nothing about it. I've wanted this forever, but each day my ignorance makes it less likely that I will ever try."

"How will you learn?"

"You can teach me. You can go first."

"I have already been."

"Then you can tell me."

"No."

"Why?!"

The lips laughed a quiet, patient laugh. When the businessman attempted to reply, he realized he had been whispering. If you were in the vicinity, you would have heard the whispers, the voices that fill all towns when the streets are crowded, yet no one is talking.

The businessman jerked his head away from the lips, spanned his hands around the hole, testing to see if the edges would sustain his weight. Again, the woman made the sound. It was an uncanny note, and the businessman's sweat turned cold, though the alley was still sweltering. He grasped the wall next to the hole and held on, his body rigid. Looking into the darkness of the chasm, juxtaposed with the faint nightlight, the businessman experienced the vertiginous sensation of one not on the brink of falling, but one who realizes he has it in his own power to remain on the ledge, or to plunge into the abyss. The compulsion to dive down was so puissant that it could have been a physical force. But the businessman stopped and looked back to the lips that released another annoyed sigh.

"What is so important?" the man said. "Huh? It's just a …"

"It's a mystery."

"And why do I have to solve it?"

"It is not to be solved."

"I thought it was a mystery."

"It is."

"And mysteries must be solved."

"Not all of them. Some must be experienced."

"That's it! I'm not interested."

"You are. You … are."

It had all begun so simply, so clearly. But from the outset of the evening, the situation had become more and more inchoate, until now it was utterly entropic. It started innocently. There was the beautiful, symbolic night; the prospect of an adventure away from the norm; the vigor, the motility to pursue the adventure because of the night one hopes to wrap his mind around; the mystery of the alley (a mystery in a mystery); the deeper mystery of the hole (a mystery in a mystery in a mystery). But now the vigor was replaced with confusion. The confusion was represented by an intense yearning to burst forth in abstract rage, cursing the world for its ill-defined secrets. But the man stopped himself, retreated, slumped down next to the hole. The moan came again.

"It doesn't matter anymore," said the man, body slackening.

"Then go."

"I will."

"No, wait."

"And?"

"*And*," she said, drawing the word out.

"Why?"

"It's what you've come to do. You must. Or ..."

"How do you know?"

"Why else would you be here?"

"There are plenty of other reasons."

"What are they?"

"Um ..."

"You'll be sorry if you don't."

"Why? Why is it so damned important?! Can you tell me? Why?! I just wanted to go for a walk. I wanted something different to happen. But now ... but now ..."

The lips gave a light laugh, their buoyancy made it all the more mocking. The businessman did not understand. He felt another explosion rising in him, yet this would be one of chaotic proportions, not at all focused as his angry speech. The man suppressed the attack. Expending so much energy to stifle the eruption, the businessman found now that his confusion was gone, replaced by despair.

The alley was stifling, but the heat was more of an unnatural heat, as if the man were feverish. He moved away from the hole, away from the light. He could no longer see anything. He stared at what he assumed to be the ground. Now, there were only voices in the dark.

"I was fine before."

"You were?"

"I was."

"You were not."

"What proof is there?"

"There are ways."

"No, there aren't. It's dangerous."

"Everything is."

Again, the businessman felt a furious passion that wished to escape through his mouth—the feeling one gets when about to be sick. But the businessman did not feel sick. This time he was impotent, unable to control his paroxysm, so he screamed a long, dolorous howl. You would have recognized it, had you heard. Anyone from the town would have recognized the howl.

"It's getting worse and worse. I can't see. It's building inside of me. I don't know what to do."

"You do."

"I don't."

"It's too bad."

"What is?"

"It."

The voice began laughing. When the laughing stopped, the businessman, on the ground, slowly spoke in an affected monotone—a voice not his own:

"I remember this story. I don't know from where. It's like it's been rattling around in my head, but I couldn't catch it. Now, I think I've got it:

"There's this man. He's walking along a road when he sees a house. Seeing the house, after walking for so long, the man thinks he'll go up, knock on the door. Hopefully, the owner will let him sit down. He could sit on the road, but he's tired of sitting on the road.

From far away, the house looks beautiful. It's a brick house with a tall, pointed roof. There's smoke coming out of the chimney. It's a pleasant house. But the closer the man gets to the house, the uglier it looks. It's rundown; the smoke might be pieces of the roofing being blown away. Only, that doesn't matter. The man wants to get to the house. It looked so good before. So, he puts his head down and keeps walking.

"When he gets to the house, the place is a shambles. The front porch is so full of holes that the man wonders if he'll fall through when he steps on it. But the road is far away, and the man wants to see the inside of the house.

"Inside, the man realizes that this is no ordinary house; when he walks through the door, the door slams behind him. He tries to open the door, but it's locked. So, he looks around. The room is completely bare except for four doors: one to the left, one straight ahead, and one to the right—the one behind him being locked. Now, the man has heard that you can get out of any maze by always turning to the left. So, he goes to the left, opens the door, walks through it, and again he's in another room filled with doors, the one behind him being locked. The man laughs, happy to be engaged in something other than walking on the road. So, he forgets his weariness and continues to take the door to the left.

"Time goes on. Who knows how many rooms he's been in? No matter what, because he heard one time that you can get out of any maze by turning left, he keeps taking the door to the left. Finally, after all those rooms, he comes to one that only has two doors: the locked one behind him and the one to the left. Without thinking, he walks directly up to the door to the left and is about to open it when he stops. He wonders why there aren't other doors to choose from. Quickly, he goes back to the door he entered through, but it's locked. There's only the one door for him, yet that's a problem. It's the same door he's always taken; why not choose it again? Only, it's not so easy this time. Something seems wrong. Like he made a mistake. Where, though? Where did he screw up? He doesn't know. All he knows is that he has one more door to go through, but because there is only one, it seems sinister.

"After much mental anguish, he opens the door and walks through. This room is narrow and short. There are no doors. When the man calmly turns around, he finds that there isn't even a door behind him. He's stuck. Marooned. So, he thinks about the road, the house, the doors. And he wonders where he went wrong."

The businessman finished speaking with a note of true finality, stood, brushed himself off, cracked his back, turned to walk away from the hole.

"It must be nice," said the voice.

"What?!"

"To know ... so well."

Waving his hands, the businessman delved deeper into the darkness.

"That's not your business. That's the wrong way," said the voice.

"I know my business; I know which way I'm going!" shouted the businessman.

"The wrong way," said the lips again.

But the businessman continued to walk in the same direction. It had to be the right way; the slope was upward and steep. Soon, however, he found that the woman must have been correct because there was a wall directly in front of him. First, it felt as if a ceiling were lowering, but now there was a wall. The businessman took no injury because he had been tramping slowly to compensate for the darkness. Leaning against the inscrutable abutment, he could see the light, so faint in the distance. The light that had revealed the abyssal hole to him. The hole. He still felt an intense yearning to run back, to jump down into it, to discover whatever he could. In the hole. If he didn't care for what he found, couldn't he get back out? Couldn't he go about his business? He could take precautions, in case the hole was too deep, to ensure his safe return. Could the woman help him?

So full of fury, the man had trouble thinking, focusing. He wanted very much to scream in anguish and frustration, but he was silent. Reluctantly, he felt his way around, trying to discover an exit.

Sliding along the walls, the wanderer had no idea where he was going. Deliberating became increasingly difficult, until it was utterly impossible. Unable to control himself any longer, he wanted to yell, "This is all your fault!" but the letters refused to right themselves. They erupted in a jumble.

His incoherent howl was met with cruel laughter. If you had been there, you would have recognized the howl. Anyone from the town would.

"There is still time," the woman said.

But her words were ignored. The wanderer stumbled ahead, he knew not where. His thoughts were so jangled, they could no longer be considered thoughts; they were electrical impulses blasting at random in his brain. Somewhere, deep down in the labyrinth of his mind, the wanderer wanted out of the anfractuous alley; he wanted to be back on the main street. Yet, it was too dark to see anything at all, and the anger that rose in him now found vent forever in his mouth.

The longer he spent roaming in what could have been a circle, the less he felt autonomous. It was now as if he were being pulled inexorably in a never-ending round, painfully thoughtless, erupting into bouts of fury. The wanderer knew not who was pulling him, nor did he have any idea why he was being pulled. Soon, the sensation was so familiar that the wanderer no longer felt drawn, felt, instead, only forward motion. It seemed that there never had been a hand to pull him with. There never had been any pulling. Nor any wandering. Never any walking. Never a woman. Never a hole. Never an alley. Never an evening. Never any light.

All was dark around him. His thoughts clouded, as if covered by an impenetrable haze, impermeable even to a calm, comfortable spotlight. He could no longer focus. He didn't know where he was going. He was tired. He had been moving forward for so long on this road, and he wanted to rest. Finally, he slumped to the ground, his back leaning on a wall.

Only it wasn't a wall. It was a door. The wooden surface seemed odd after rubbing against the brick. Still in darkness, the man turned around, hands grazing over the portal to he knew not where, until he found the knob, which he used to lift himself up before he pushed the door open.

When he slid through the doorway, all remained black. He fell to the ground. A barrage of epithets escaped his lips. But nothing else is to be expected.

This morning, in your town, Fuck You Bob died. Everyone was talking about it. You were jarred by the news because, just last night, you experienced such a bizarre scene involving Bob. On account of your moment with the homeless man, you found yourself thinking of the many times you have seen Bob raving outside of the dilapidated brick building on the main street. Often, you found that you hadn't even realized he was there, until suddenly he appeared as if from nowhere and everywhere. But such is the case with most vagabonds. You never look for them. Sometimes, even when they are directly in front of you, you find that you can't see them—they are ethereal beings only called into existence by the right minds, the right pair of eyes; then, one day, as you are strolling along, there they are, just as they've always been.

With Fuck You Bob, however, you grew curious. You found yourself, this morning, asking about him. Your investigation led you to a very old woman's house. You asked the old woman how long Bob had been raving on the main street: she said as long as she'd been in the city. You asked if she knew what he was like before: the woman said she knew him before. You asked what happened, how did he end up like this? She said that he turned and left. He turned left. Left and left and left. She cackled. She rocked back and forth repeating the word "left." Never right, he went left. He left.

You took leave of the deranged old lady and walked back to the main street, right to the spot where Bob used to sit, staring blindly ahead. Outside of a dilapidated brick building.

You now sit across the street from his spot, gazing forth. As if he were appearing for you and you alone, the ghost of Fuck You Bob suddenly materializes much as he was in life. He stares forward, directly at you. He raves. You see him walk up to part of the building, his back to you. He curses the wall. He shrieks at the wall. He is old and blind, and he shrieks at the wall. It appears as if he is shaking a door by the handle, a door that is locked. But you cannot see a door. You see only a wall. In despair, Bob returns to his usual spot, looking blindly ahead at you, yet seeing only darkness.

And then he disappears.

In the wind you hear a string of epithets. But nothing else is to be expected.

TO BUILD A FIRE
... IN SPACE

While floating along, the first thought to hit his mind: How chilly it is! Extremely chilly. Frigid. Arctic. Antarctic, even. The man had certainly not experienced such depths of mercury back home. But where was home? Was home located in a tropical clime, making the previous assertion of inexperience unsurprising? (Might "depths," therefore, be the wrong word?) Or did he hail from a far northerly or far southerly area, making the "depths of mercury" statement a startling revelation since such a person ought to be acclimatized to a frosty atmosphere? How truly glacial it must be if *he* is getting chilblains! Yet, the man's thoughts did not drift to his origins. He merely thought of the cold.

How to get warm? The obvious answer: fire. Fire makes people warm, and, therefore, the man would

TO BUILD A FIRE ... IN SPACE

build a fire. Which should be easy. To build a fire, one only needs wood, paper for kindling (although dry leaves would do), a lighter or match (flint and steel would also work (and if it came down to it, one could rub two sticks together—which, mind you, was good enough for the Pioneers when they were in the same situation (were the Pioneers ever in *this particular* situation?))), and stones to contain the blaze. Roasting marshmallows would be nice, but if one is to roast marshmallows:

> 1.) One ought to invite his friends because
>> A.) It is damned depressing roasting marshmallows by yourself, and
>> B.) One can only roast marshmallows while telling ghost stories, but if ghost stories are to be told:
>>> (1.) One should know *which* ghost stories to tell to the group gathered; for instance, if there are children, the ghost stories should be scary in a very simplistic way so the young'-ins will ultimately go to sleep; whereas, if there are adults present, the ghost stories should either be terrifying or hilarious or filled with sexual innuendoes (nudge, nudge, har, har and all that which makes people reply, "'Nuff said," although more properly it should be, "'Nough said), and
>>> (2.) One should recognize which of the group members are the best tellers, in turn giving *them* the utmost attention, while cracking jokes and

providing ludicrous sidebars during the stories told by those who are not as skilled;

2.) One ought to know the proper type of stick to roast a marshmallow on: Do you use sharpened sticks from the woods or those steel implements that resemble great, long steak stabbers from the grocery store (they even have ones that rotate mechanically! (but then one must think of batteries and battery chargers and biodegradable vs. the cheapest damned batteries one can find, and we definitely don't want to go off on that track)), and while speaking of roasting marshmallows, the topic of s'mores must be broached, for there will certainly be those amongst the invited who will wonder why the camp-leader has decided to skimp on the chocolate and graham crackers and, thus, only provided marshmallows to angle over the flames: Do you want to be the kind of person who leaves his fellow fire afficionados unfulfilled? One assumes not, no matter where you might be, but one also needs to think about providing hot dogs, s'mores being *technically* a dessert food and, although occasionally tempting, most personages (folks, shall we say?) do not want to eat *only* dessert foods; but when supplying hot dogs, one needs to remember to supply regular hot dogs, kosher hot dogs, turkey dogs (for those who do not eat beef), and soy hot dogs (for those who do not eat meat), and, needless to say (but said anyhow), mustard, catsup, relish, cheese, sauerkraut, chili, potato chips, coleslaw, potato salad, soda pop, beer, and you need to make sure that the children do not stab each other with the grocery store marshmallow sticks (that spin mechanically) while devouring the chocolate and throwing the marshmallows and graham crackers at each other (also possibly dumping the potato salad into the coleslaw) and that the children do not drink the beer (or dump it into the potato salad or coleslaw); finally, to build a fire, one needs to make sure that there is plenty of space. You do not want to burn the entire forest down. You do not want the children to fall into the flames. You do not want the drunken adults to see if they can jump over the fire.

But, as long as the man could gather together these few accoutrements, floating along, he could have a fire. Which would keep him warm. Because it was awfully ... well, there was a bit of a nip in the air, no doubt about it.

So, where to get started? The man certainly didn't know the area, so finding a grocery store where all the food and mechanically spinning steak stabbers could be purchased might be a problem. Which might mean no marshmallows, let alone chocolate or graham crackers for s'mores. Soy hot dogs, right out. And there were no pay telephones (having misplaced his cell phone somewhere (would this be considered a Roaming call? (one always needs to be marking the Roaming areas in order to guard against exorbitant charges))), so it might be difficult to contact anyone (but without any marshmallows or mechanically spinning steak stabbers, would it even be appropriate to call one's friends (not to mention the complete lack of s'mores materials)?). Also, to be perfectly honest, there weren't any stones around to contain the fire; thus, it might be dangerous to build one in the first place. Which in itself might be a moot point because, well, to put it plainly, there didn't appear to be any trees. And without trees there aren't any leaves to start the fire with, any branches to get the fire going, any logs to sustain the conflagration, any forest to protect against the possible ravages of the flames, any pulp-paper companies to manufacture paper that will carry the story of how the man burned the entire place down because of improper containment. What there was plenty of, however: Space. Space in which to build a fire.

There was space.

And oh! the man just remembered. He had brought his lighter along—flint and steel be damned. So, he flicked the lighter. And for a brief instant, he saw a spark. Or thought he did. And then, again, he wondered anew what one needed to build a fire. And this time he realized what was missing. In order to build a fire, the first thing one needs is

THE FIRST CIRCUMNAVIGATOR

The history books, those august receptacles of Absolute Truth, inform us—and why should we question them?—that the first person to circumnavigate the earth was not Juan Sebastián Elcano of Spain, nor Enrique of Malacca, and certainly not Antonio Pigafetta of Italy, but, under the direction of those tomes of Veracity, the name listed, invoked, the name commanded even, is Ferdinand Magellan of Portugal. It is a fact we are required to memorize in grade school, one we unlikely forget. Perhaps we also remember that Magellan, although Portuguese, sailed under the Spanish flag. Doubtful we recall the reason: Magellan fell out of favor with Manuel I, king of Portugal, for taking leave without permission after being wounded in the knee in Morocco, for (allegedly) illegally trading with

Moors, and for other (some say petty, trumped up, others claim major) crimes brought by whispers into his majesty's court. This attribution as the First Circumnavigator is thanks to the tireless efforts of Maximilianus Transylvanus, who published the first report on the expedition, entitled *De Moluccis Insulis* (1523). Transylvanus was not on the voyage. His information, then, was collected by interviewing fifteen of the eighteen survivors, those few remaining from the 237 who first set sail on five ships. Deeply enamored with their fallen admiral, the sailors and passengers passed their veneration on to Transylvanus, who became obsessed with Magellan. In their reports, the extant explorers had already exaggerated the Portuguese's character, and Transylvanus, assuming the crew were being faithful, exaggerated more so—Magellan's oratorical power, his conversational wit, his stately mien, his handsome visage, his physical strength, his refined tastes in music, painting, sculpture, poetry, clothing, wine, his devotion to God, his patriotism (although Portugal had slighted him). Of Magellan, Transylvanus made a pious Achilles, a humble Odysseus, a spurned Aeneas, a contemporary Jason who had led his Argonauts around the entire earth, hence the reason, throughout the monograph, he is referred to as, "Magellan, the First Circumnavigator." Transylvanus even includes Magellan's heroic death in the Battle of Mactan in the Philippines at the hands of "savages," the "savages" swarming over the Portuguese, the admiral hacking into their ranks to save his crew (before Jason, now Roland), the rest of the sailors broken, forced to flee, leaving the body of the hero finally overwhelmed by the enemy (even he could not last against such an onslaught), yes, leaving the body of the epic hero behind never to be seen again, sixteen months before the *Victoria* returned to Spain full of spices from the Moluccas. For the number of pages dedicated to it, however, the remainder of the voyage might as well have comprised languidly steering the ship to the shore of Sanlúcar de Barrameda, a mere fifteen-thousand or so miles. During the interview process, there were only three survivors that Transylvanus was unable to speak with: Juan Sebastián Elcano, Enrique of Malacca, and Antonio Pigafetta (more on him later). Concerning the first, whereas the crew were enamored with their admiral, they were disdainful of the once-mutinous Captain Elcano, a disdain they passed on to Transylvanus. Furthermore, upon his return, Elcano immediately began preparations for another voyage, as if the journey just completed had been a prosaic affair, another notch in the belt of a perpetual traveler. Fully occupied by his endeavors, Elcano agreed to various appointments with Transylvanus, only to cancel each meeting, until the time finally arrived for the captain to depart. Already contemptuous of Elcano, Transylvanus thought of slighting the Spaniard by making a villain of him, or a comical foil; instead, he snubbed the Spaniard by mentioning him but twice throughout the monograph. Dismissing the lout, Transylvanus now thirsted for more knowledge of his epic hero. Upon discovering the name of another surviving crew member, a crew member very close to Magellan, one Enrique of Malacca, Transylvanus published (to him, the incomplete) *De Moluccis Insulis*, and set out for Cebu, Enrique's last-known whereabouts.

Later, Elcano would get his due. With the publication of Antonio Pigafetta's *First Voyage Around the World*

(1525), the record was, supposedly, set straight. Unlike Transylvanus, Pigafetta was on the journey, having paid a large sum of money to sail with Magellan. Unlike Transylvanus, Pigafetta did not have to rely on unsubstantiated claims made by sailors over a year after the death of the Portuguese. Pigafetta obtained his information firsthand, keeping a journal to document the trek. Furthermore, Pigafetta favored neither Magellan nor Elcano, truthfully appearing to be indifferent to both of them. His tome, therefore, cites Elcano, undeniably, as the first to circumnavigate the globe. Disinterested in this agon, however, Pigafetta also proves that Magellan, having been to the Spice Islands before (where he purchased his slave and translator, a man called "Henrich"), had crossed all of the meridians of the world by the time of his death, but not in a continuous one-way trip. Yet, there are two problems with Pigafetta's account. 1.) Being of great length, the entire manuscript was never published, and, in fact, the original draft was later lost in Paris. 2.) If Transylvanus' monograph aggrandized his hero, Magellan, Pigafetta's account aggrandized his own hero, Antonio Pigafetta. Having spent the majority of his waking hours with Magellan and Elcano, indeed, Pigafetta transcribes their accomplishments accurately, but almost as an afterthought. The focus of *First Voyage Around the World*, then, is Pigafetta's experiences: first sighting of new lands, seasickness, encounters with native women and girls, meals, moods, discussions, storms—all of these occurrences and many more happened first and foremost to Antonio Pigafetta. When others are included in the Italian's account of the circumnavigation, they are introduced as and always remain minor characters, including Magellan and Elcano. The minor characters, then, are auditors of the wisdom and grandiloquence of Antonio Pigafetta; like Plato's seconds to Socrates, the minor characters are only present to help further illustrate Pigafetta's intelligence, wisdom, wit, and taste. Elcano, in this account, is neither made a hero nor a villain, nor is he slighted, but contrarily is shown as a determined man, a driven man, one prone to bouts of choler (as evidenced by his former mutiny), but a good person, nonetheless; the factuality of this account is unknown, for elsewhere Pigafetta includes Henrich in with the dead after the Battle of Mactan, only later to discover that Henrich left the ship at Cebu before the Battle of Mactan took place. Undeterred in his self-confidence, self-concerned, self-centered, self-contained, and self-satisfied, Pigafetta names Elcano as the captain of the *Victoria* when the ship completes the voyage, but it is quite obvious that Pigafetta believes that *he*, himself, should be the one remembered as the First Circumnavigator, for without Antonio Pigafetta, the journey could never have been completed, assumedly because everyone would have died of boredom or despair without him.

Throughout the previous two accounts, there has been a shadowy character who now figures into our tale: Enrique of Malacca, also known as Henrich. For along with Magellan, Elcano, perhaps even Pigafetta, Enrique is another candidate for the title of First Circumnavigator. Kidnapped by Sumatran slave traders, he was later purchased by Magellan in a Malaccan market (where he was baptized and given his Christian name, his birth name being lost to the ages); Enrique, after sale, would work as an interpreter and personal servant to the Portuguese. Taken to Portugal and then Spain, the slave accompanied the admiral on his great journey. Throughout, Magellan treated Enrique as an equal, and even put a provision in his will granting freedom to Enrique upon the death of the Portuguese. Others were not as open-minded. Although uncertain, Transylvanus, in the only passage where he mentions Enrique, says that Juan Serrano, original captain of the *Santiago*, maliciously and relentlessly abused Enrique. Some even believe this oppression led Enrique to mastermind the massacre of Mactan, a plan that, if plotted by Enrique, backfired, for there Magellan died, not Serrano. Pigafetta, on the other hand, blames Duarte Barbosa for the massacre, but few give credence to this account. Nevertheless, Enrique was abused, and when the fleet reached Cebu, he escaped into the custody of Rajah Humabon, the king of the island. At this point, our account can rely only on conjecture, for Enrique's birthplace, along with his actual name, are lost to the ages. If Enrique was from Cebu, when the fleet arrived on the island, Enrique had circumnavigated the earth. If, however, Enrique was not from Cebu, but from an island to the West, he could have returned before Elcano set foot on the Spanish shore, sixteen months later.

In an attempt to learn more about Magellan, Transylvanus searched for Enrique, hunted for the interpreter to the great Magellan. On Cebu, Enrique could not be found, but Transylvanus was informed that, certainly, he was living in Malacca. On Malacca, he could not be found, but Transylvanus was informed that, certainly, he could be found in the Maluku Islands. On the Maluku Islands, he could not be found, but Transylvanus was informed that, certainly, he could be found in the Malay Archipelago. Transylvanus scoured every island in the Malay Archipelago, but still, he could not locate Enrique; he could never locate Enrique. During this hunt, however, a fear grew in the heart of the questor: What if he found that Enrique had actually completed the circumnavigation before Admiral Magellan? What if his myths were dispelled? Later, on an island so small that it had no name of its own, Transylvanus, racked by fever, found the only link he would ever have to Magellan's interpreter; but the man was old, possibly senile, and rarely spoke. Transylvanus, who had mas-tered the Cebuano tongue by now, related what he had learned about Magellan, what he had written in *De Mol-uccis Insulis*, what Pigafetta had written in *First Voyage Around the World*, what he had undergone to find En-rique of Malacca. Transylvanus then fell into a coma, where he surely would have died without the help of the old man. Upon recovery, Transylvanus thanked his caretaker, and left the islands, returning to Spain, then to Transylvania, his homeland, where he spent the rest of his life. As an elder himself, one day, Transylvanus suddenly recalled a tale—where he heard it, he could not remember; who told it to him was equally myster-ious; and, after transcribing it to the best of his ability, Transylvanus asked his nurse to take him to where he could see the horizon. The nurse, dumbfounded, asked why. But her question would never be answered, for Maximilianus Transylvanus was dead; and the piece of paper he held in his hands did nothing to explain the situation.

ANDREW FARKAS

The Tale of Magellan and the Horizon

Amongst the many lies of life, and thankfully there are many, one tells of an explorer named Magellan who sailed for Spain to find a Pacific route to the Spice Islands, as they are known in the West, and the Maluku Islands, as they are known in the East. The lie was not invented after the fact. The admiral's crew also believed that their mission was to find a commercial passage, and having the orders from the holy Roman emperor, Charles V, no one doubted them. Magellan, himself, knew of this belief, but kept silent, for unlike the epic by Transylvanus, and equally unlike the chronicle of Pigafetta, Magellan was mute. He spoke not a word, intoned not a single syllable his entire life. Being mute, he could tell no lies, and when the ruler of Spain commissioned Magellan with the use of five of his ships (*Victoria, Concepción, Trinidad, San Antonio, Santiago*), having spoken of nothing save the need for a route to the Spice Islands, it was assumed, when Magellan gave his humble bow, that he had accepted the mission. Once aboard ship, Magellan spent his waking hours on deck looking out across the water; rarely could he be found in his quarters. And whenever orders were required, the Portuguese merely pointed to the horizon. At the outset, upon finding they were being pursued by ships sent by King Manuel of Portugal (upset with Magellan for supposedly assisting Spain), the crew asked what should be done? Magellan gave not a pause and pointed to the horizon. When the five ships reached the Cape Verde islands, after eluding Manuel's pursuit, the crew asked for a bearing, and Magellan, again, pointed to the horizon. When they reached Rio de Janeiro, Brazil, after

THE FIRST CIRCUMNAVIGATOR

crossing the Atlantic Ocean, the crew, once more, requested their orders, and the admiral once more gave not a pause and pointed to the horizon. Along the way, two ships were lost, there was a mutiny (unsuccessful), and the fleet had to persevere as they dealt with the stagnant waters of the South Pacific, but still, forever and always, the only order from Magellan was to point to the horizon. Once in the Philippines, the crews of Magellan's fleet became embroiled in the Battle of Mactan, thanks to the king of Cebu, and perhaps because of the abuse of Enrique of Malacca. During the battle, as described by Antonio Pigafetta, the great Magellan fell. The men were crushed at the loss of their beloved admiral. And although he had not circumnavigated the globe, he had completed his official mission of finding a commercial route to Asia. Only one man realized that Magellan had not succeeded in accomplishing his own, personal mission, but instead had failed, and that man would go on to be one of the first circumnavigators of the earth: Juan Sebastián Elcano. For Elcano saw the Portuguese when he fell in battle, and he saw the explorer, in his dying gasp, reach for the horizon with his bare hand, as if he could grasp it, as if he were about to grasp it, only to have it finally and cruelly elude his clutches.

Yet, what are we to make of Magellan? Amongst the reports of Transylvanus and Pigafetta we find gross inaccuracies, self-serving subjectivity, entertaining lies. Enrique, or Henrich, has a different story. Enrique claims Transylvanus located him, though Transylvanus was near death with fever at the time. Deranged, demented, the seeker demanded Enrique to explain, to explain everything about Magellan. Enrique explained that the Portuguese dealt with anything close at hand apathetically, including the unsuccessful mutiny at Puerto San Julián. When one might expect righteous indignation (the admiral's command had been violently challenged), there were only what appeared to be bows to protocol, for Magellan executed naught save one or two men (Henrich could not recall if both Gaspar de Quesada, original captain of the *Concepción, and* Luis de Mendoza, original captain of the *Victoria*, had been put to death, or if it was only Quesada), marooned but two (Juan de Cartagena and Padre Sánchez de la Reina), and pardoned one—Elcano!; furthermore, the admiral did not beam with joy and pride at his crew's loyalty and admiration during the brief insurrection, for Magellan's only passion was the horizon. Nowhere was this more apparent than in the still waters of the South Pacific. Here, with the ships stationary, Magellan stormed back and forth on the deck, emphatically pointing to that visual meridian, trying, for the only time, to scream at his officers and crewmen, impotent to do so, his lips madly communicating nothing, his *voice* coming out as a rasping screech of no known language.

Since he could not speak, and since he rarely wrote anything more than a terse command, no one knows whether he were equally dismissive of everything at hand, or if he were equally accepting of everything at hand. If he was equally dismissive, he wished to go to the horizon because of his distaste for his surroundings; if he was equally accepting, then he wished merely to gain more experience and knew that experience was to be found beyond a point unattainable. But there is a third possibility: perhaps Magellan accepted everything because he had already dismissed it; perhaps Magellan, knowing of no reality other than this, set an absurd goal for himself, a goal as absurd as being trapped in a reality not at all constructed for you.

An addendum: Throughout the voyage, the crew of the five ships under Magellan's command believed they knew their purpose, namely that they were in search of a commercial route to Asia and that they were in control of their situation. Content with their circumstances, the sailors gave all the credit to their mysterious admiral, for certainly he was to thank. In actuality, they had no idea what their purpose was, and they had no control over their situation. Instead, Magellan had all of the control and only he knew the purpose, but he never spoke, leaving his crew utterly nescient to his actual goal, remaining silent until his death. Immediately following the demise of Magellan, Elcano took command of the *Victoria*, had the *Concepción* burned (for there were not enough sailors to man two ships), and, when the crew asked for their orders, Elcano spoke not a word. Gave not a pause. And only pointed to the horizon. Later Elcano, much like Magellan before him, would die on another voyage around the globe, for neither the Spaniard nor the Portuguese could ever reach that which was in sight, that which was right in front of them, and only on cloudy days when men's minds are full of delusion do we ever get any closer to it.

A ROGUE DEPARTMENT COURSE OFFERING

ROGUE 101: UNSITUATED WRITING

Description of the Class

This class will cover the finer points of writing from no known situation. Here, you will never quite grasp such topics as experiencing a limitless vacuum, a nigh-infinite white space, an always-changing plane developed by those who can see all thirty or so dimensions of the multiverse discussed in the Everett many-worlds interpretation of quantum mechanics. You will be asked to write about these unfathomable experiences using not computers, not typewriters, not pens, not pencils, not markers, not crayons, and certainly not paper, not papyrus, nor any other accepted writing utensil or surface, except that each paper should be either two- or four-hundred pages long, the opposite of what you turn in being the correct length. Furthermore, you will be expected to write only in dead languages, unless you know a dead language, in which case you can only write in Klingon, unless you know Klingon, in which case you will certainly be mocked, and then be expected to write in the language spoken by those who cannot be named who are from an equally unnameable planet. Should you learn the name of those who cannot be named, and if you learn the name of the unnameable planet, you will have, in a sense, situated yourself, and will not only immediately fail the class, but will also fail at everything thereafter.

Location of the Class

Our meetings will not take place on the sixth Monday of each month (unless the twelfth of Never falls on the sixth Monday of one of the months, in which case, we will also not meet on that day), and said meetings will or will not be held on the thirteenth floor of any hotel that has a thirteenth floor, will certainly not be held anywhere near this campus, and should you find where the class is being held, not only will you fail the course, not only will you fail at life, but you will also be subject to fines and a prison sentence meted out by those who cannot be named on their unnameable planet.

Books for the Class

Potential books that won't be used for the class are *The Princess Bride* by S. Morgenstern (not the version by William Goldman), Pierre Menard's version of *Don Quixote* (should you bring to class the Cervantes version, that means you found where we're meeting ...), any of the books found in Stanisław Lem's *A Perfect Vacuum*, *Necronomicon*, Oolon Colluphid's *Where God Went Wrong*, Nathan Glass' *The Book of Human Folly*, W. P. Mayhew's *Nebuchadnezzar*, T. Azimuth Schwitters' *Eventualism*, and all of the works by Kilgore Trout. None of these books can be found at the bookstore, nor can they be found at Barnes & Noble, Myopic in Chicago, Powell's in Portland, the Strand in New York, nor any other bookstore for that matter, but this shouldn't daunt you because none of these books exist anyhow.

Sample Paper from the Class

Can you see it? Can you understand it? Can you imagine it? There you are. Floating through a limitless vacuum, unable to see, unable to breathe, unable to feel your atmosphere, completely cut off from your surroundings to the point where you're not even certain if you are in the nigh-infinite white space, or if you're in the ever-changing plane, which may sometimes look like a nigh-infinite white space, or if you're hallucinating both while gliding through a limitless vacuum. How long until you get used to this sensation that is a complete lack of sensations? Are you used to it already? Are you situated? Good. That means you can't write about it.

Grades

One student said about this class: Some people believe you pass this class by not taking it. This isn't true because everyone is always taking it since you sign up for it by not signing up for it. Some people, therefore, say that you pass this class by signing up for it. But the only place where you can sign up for this course is at any location where the class is being held, meaning before you've signed up for it, you've immediately failed (in more ways than one). The actual solution is you cannot escape this class. You can only hope you don't find yourself in it any time soon.

IS THIS THE SHIP OF THESEUS?

> We accept reality easily, perhaps because we intuit that nothing is real.
> —Jorge Luis Borges, "The Immortal"

When I was younger, I was frequently left alone, my parents not being the overprotective type. With so much time to myself, I was able, because of a ruminative bent and a sedentary nature—even at such an early age—to explore my own mind, daydreaming, staring at the pictures which, for reasons unknown now and forever to me, hung on my wall: a Greek trireme and a print of Chuck Close's painting *Lucas*. In this—I shall not say *idyllic*, but perhaps *halcyon*, though one may also posit *bathetic*—environment, I spent the whole (or perhaps *remainder* would be more appropriate) of my childhood not quite isolated, for there were my loving mother and my loving father who provided all the companionship I required, bringing my sum total of life experience at that age to an often private, though by no means lonely or alienated, existence focused on the operations of my own mentality. I never suspected how this period would be brought to an end.

One day I felt the need for physical activity and, therefore, decided to help my family by chopping wood. We lived in a rural area; we had a great deal of land with plenty of timber. Now, I wasn't asked, and to be frank had never been asked, nor was I expected by anyone, though the only people I knew were my mother and father, since I was so young, to chop wood. But I'd seen my dad do it and thought I'd give it a try. Grabbing my grandfather's axe, a tool so old that the double-blade had been replaced innumerable times and the handle, too, innumerable times, I thought something like, *The strength of my lineage will assist me*, only not that exactly on account of my age, so maybe more like, *My family is strong!*, a ringing endorsement pulsing through my mind for my genealogical tree as I went out to work.

Our immediate backyard was completely flat for a good fifty meters and then broke into a declivity, at the bottom of which was a stand of cypress, at the top of which was the woodpile where I stood chopping the felled trees into logs, the logs into more manageable pieces, the pieces into smaller chunks that could fit easily into the stove my father had installed in our basement in order to heat part of the house. He said it saved on the cost of propane. Being so young, and being unaccustomed to sustained action, perhaps because I spent so much time staring at the paintings on my wall and daydreaming, I got tired quickly. But since I suddenly saw myself as a woodsman protecting his family from an impending blizzard, I found, deep within my person, a reserve of heretofore undiscovered energy, though to be honest, I had not gone in search of it previously, which allowed me to push myself on, even when I was dizzy with exhaustion.

Much of what happened next had to be told to me. And to this day, I'm not sure if I can trust the sources, as you will soon understand.

Supposedly, I was spotted chopping wood from a great distance by *someone*, this questionable person having rounded the house and entered the backyard, or so I'm told, just *in the nick of time*, to use the clichéd words of my self-selected chroniclers. I've been informed on many occasions the *someone* was my father, but I doubt this seriously. Whoever it was that did see me claims I hefted Grandfather's axe, as before in my many successful strikes at the log, but this time instead of the tool soaring above in a true arc, the flat of the blade crashed into my forehead, knocking me backward, and likely immediately unconscious (if I can believe this story), the episode ending, in the telling anyway, as the axe fell to the ground, me collapsing, rolling to the bottom of the hill, where I crashed head first (how could that *someone* know from *Their* vantage point?) into a tree.

I have been told my *parents* were *mortified*. My *ersatz* father, as he unfortunately put it, *hollered bloody murder* to my equally ersatz mother, who, supposedly and without pause, picked up the phone and called the paramedics. As I am again informed, the ambulance arrived in minutes, but the time *felt like an eternity*, to quote more of Their absurd lines, because my dad believed he couldn't touch me for fear my neck were broken and any wrong move would lead to further injury. Once I was secured by the paramedics, the disreputable storytellers allow that I was *whisked off* to a certain location, no one ever specified where, making it a very *un*certain location, and that from this ambiguous place, I was taken by helicopter (*a helicopter?*) to a (yokel term) *big-city* hospital.

It might be that none of this is true. I was unconscious the entire time.

Being a child, what followed was confusing to me. I woke in a strange place, surrounded by unrecognizable people and imposing machines that made alarming sounds. There were so many doctors and specialists I could never remember any of their names, and so, when I could see, finally, I had one of my attendants lean in close. His or her name was Dr. Fregoli. From there on out, I called all of the medical staff Dr. Fregoli, which made everyone believe Dr. Fregoli was my favorite. This was far from the truth.

After what seemed *like an eternity*, to use phrasing They would understand all too well, of tests and treatments and operations, I was finally, and not without a little ceremony, sent away from the hospital. I say *sent away* and not *sent home* on purpose. ...

Even though I'd been *on the mend* for so long, the people who *spirited* me off were still solicitous, my ersatz father driving as slowly as possible so as not to upset my precarious condition. I realized almost immediately what was going on. The people who were taking me away from the hospital, They resembled my parents, certainly. My hulking father was still rumpled, always looking like he'd slept in a wadded-up pile of the clothes he was wearing. No matter how much he combed his hair, it still looked unkempt, a mass of reddish brown that concluded in two mammoth lupine lambchops but which also appeared over his hazel eyes and the rest of his body. My mother, quite the opposite, was prim and tiny, her skin an ethereal pallor that showed blue and green veins, a roadmap leading nowhere, her hair dyed raven black.

The effect of the simulation was striking. But these were not my parents. Maybe it was because I was still tired from the hospital, but I wasn't afraid. I was even bold enough to ask who They were, though all I heard, in my half-daze, were three words that told me more about my situation than the impostors probably intended. They said *concussion* and *brain injury*, so I knew, right off, what story They were using, putting me in a privileged position. Strange They were so incompetent.

Once we'd arrived at our destination, my ersatz father carried me into a house, deposited me onto a bed, and there I instantly fell asleep, something I wasn't allowed to do at the beginning of my stay in the hospital. How long I slept, I have no idea. What machinations were put in place while I slumbered, I know not. All I do know is that, when I rose, I immediately saw the first mistake in Their plan. My Chuck Close painting of Lucas Samaras was now a confusion of colors that formed no face I could discern, more closely resembling, I now realize, a Jackson Pollock. Walking through the house, I quickly understood that, although this was a masterful copy, it was not my home. This was not my room. This was not my hallway. This was not my bathroom. This was not my father's library.

IS THIS THE SHIP OF THESEUS?

Yet, being ignorant still as to the point of this hoax, I did not flee in disgust, in case I was being watched, the simulacrum of my father's study as his actual bibliothèque, before the *accident*, was one of my normal haunts. There I found all the same books in all the same places. While looking at the shelves, wondering what I was going to do, wondering what They wanted from me, wondering what They intended to do to me, I happened upon a leather-bound tome I'd studied with interest many times before. It was my family's ancestor chart and history.

The chart itself was inked on vellum (my actual father being, perhaps, too enamored of that which was, at least in appearance, ancient) and doubled up many times in the manner of maps. Opened before me, I recalled what my father had said, that our genealogy resembled, in myriad ways, the Lone Cypress near Monterey, a place that seemed fantastic, making our family unique via this connection to something not of our world. I tried to hold that image in my mind, of the macrocarpa growing from the cliff, sprouting from ground so inhospitable, thriving—healthy and green—in land truly opposed to life, while I read through the ancestry, a paragraph or so about each member, leading back to the most august branch, only to find that part of Their plan, whatever it was, included crippling me with headaches. The world, as I thought then, in my juvenile mind, was being shaken apart by a continual drumbeat, and soon, everything would, without fail, disintegrate, the cliff crumbling, the tree breaking, sliding, succumbing at last if I did not hold it all together. I fought through the shock waves, unwilling to be the cause of the Lone Cypress' demise, experiencing the same anxiety of anticipation I always felt as I got closer and closer to my favorite entry, the most famous person in my family, cranial agony increasing, until I reached the page, and reality once again went smooth and placid, though a slight pain persisted, though in the end, the tree was destroyed anyway.

Joseph Capgras was no longer there. He had been replaced. In *his place* was a Mrs. D—, whose name I withhold for reasons of privacy, as I do not wish to make of her a historical pariah, seeing as she is blameless in this endeavor to prune my lineage's most venerable limb, a man who was hailed in my family on a daily basis, a man who was used as proof of our scientific and intellectual *eclat*, a man who was not just a *limb*, but the very *trunk* itself. The fact that I *found* this information *by chance* right as the shock waves *ceased* was why I couldn't tell anyone what had happened to me. Because if I did tell someone, anyone, They would merely return me to Dr. Fregoli; if I demanded a new physician, I would be reintroduced to Dr. Fregoli; if I asked for a second opinion, it would be the same as the first, for the doctor who would deliver it would be Dr. Fregoli; if I refused to take my medicine, if I pretended to be well, a specialist would be sent in to monitor me, to see if I were actually taking my medicine, to see if I were actually well, and that doctor would be Dr. Fregoli; if I fled, I would be pursued by Dr. Fregoli; if I found a band of outsiders who knew of and were battling against the grand conspiracy, who were overjoyed, who were proud to have me, me, the one spoken of, a comrade in their revolution, me, a person who could be depended on, me, possibly the one who would change the course of the action, me ... but first, allow us to present you to our leader, our leader, a great, just this way, you're gonna love, and who ... who would be standing before me, head shaking slowly, reaching out to take my pulse, saying, "You're not well?" And there would be more tests, and there would be more operations, and, in the end, I would once again be sent away with charlatans to a counterfeit home by whom?

I would be sent away by Dr. Fregoli.

I was trapped. How could I escape? They were all in on it. And They were giving me this terrible headache. On the floor of my ersatz father's library, I passed out. When I woke, I stood on shaky legs, head in my hands. The pain had subsided. And other than a feeling of general weakness, I was fine. Fine. When I opened my eyes. When I could see. Finally. I found I was in front of a mirror. Understanding that I was surrounded. On all sides. By impostors and simulacra. I walked to the one person I felt I could depend on—myself.

In front of the mirror, I looked, with confidence, at the person I was, content that there was someone who would always, no matter what, be there for me. But looking at my reflection in the glass, I began to wonder. I knew my parents had been replaced. I knew my house had been replaced. I knew everything in the house, yes, even Grandfather's axe had been replaced. But what about me? Who was to say that *I* had not been replaced ...?

Oh, I am sorry. I did not mean to deceive you. But thinking on it, none of this story happened to me. Why did I tell it? I do not know. Where did it take place? Elsewhere. *Where?* A place I've never been. Whom did it concern? Someone else. *Whom?* I don't know that, either. Then *why* did I tell it? Because even though I've never met him, even though I still don't know him, I feel we shared the same life, if only for a while, somewhere in the mythic past. ...

With the speed of a child he ran out of the library it was far worse than he'd imagined and fleeing was the only option fleeing from every impostor he was trying to run from the worst not thinking about where he was going in order to throw himself off his own trail until he stopped in front of the trireme. It was the ship of Theseus. The picture was not, as one might expect, of Theseus leading his men home. Instead, it showed the craft being renovated. Used only when it carried the Athenian envoys to the festival of Apollo at Delos, the vessel spent the rest of the year anchored in the harbor, supposed proof that the legend of Theseus was not a legend at all, though the ship, preserved for over a millennium, had been refurbished so many times nothing of the original existed any longer. Next to the trireme was *Lucas*. A force seemed to radiate out from him, or perhaps into him, as if his body were transforming, as if, who knows?, he were being bombarded by shock waves, and after they shook him apart, he would continue on as someone or something else ...?

It could be.

But I leave you with this: There are those who believe, indeed truly believe, that all of their cells are replaced every seven years, that their entire corporeal existence metamorphoses completely in that time. This is only actually true in the body. The cells in the brain are never replaced. The ones that die are gone forever. The ones that live have always been with you broadcasting myths from other times.

WRITTEN WITH YOU SITTING NEXT TO ME

Dear —,
How are you I am fine.
As I write this, you are sitting next to me. You see me writing. You see me writing this letter that is intended for you. That I will send to you in the future after you and I have parted ways. There is nothing that I can say in this letter that I cannot say right now by turning my head in your direction and speaking. I could even read this letter out loud to you since it is intended for you and perhaps elicit a laugh, and that would begin our conversation, which would lead to my stopping this letter and speaking with you, saying the things out loud

that I am now writing, which would perhaps be even easier. In the future, when you read this letter, you will remember sitting next to me, here in the past, and wonder why I wrote you a letter instead of merely talking to you. You will remember me staring intently at the page, as if what I wrote was of the utmost significance, and you will remember not talking to me because you assumed that you would be interrupting something of importance either to myself or to someone else. But if you would have spoken to me, breaking my train of thought in what I wanted to say to you, then it would've been no different than if we were having a conversation, and you had interrupted me in order to ask for a clearer explanation or to interject something of possible importance or at least of possible interest to us both. Only, you did not interrupt, you were perfectly polite and allowed me to continue writing my unnecessary letter that you are now reading, there in the future, probably wondering what it was I had to say that had to be written while you sat next to me wondering what it was that I was so intent on writing. If you would've interrupted early in the going only to ask what I was writing, I would've responded truthfully and said, "Why, I'm writing you a letter." Probably you would've laughed, not believing me, perhaps even thanking me for being so considerate as to write you a letter to show that I was thinking of you as you sat next to me there in the past, where I wrote this letter that you are now reading there in the future, which is your present. You may've even said that it was about goddamned time I had written you a letter since I had promised to write, and up until that point, in the past where you were sitting right next to me, I had not followed through on my promise; I had, so to speak, reneged. And if this were the case, perhaps in the future (your present), where you are reading this letter, although my present is the past where I am writing this letter as I sit next to you and you wait for me to finish so our meeting can begin, so our conversation can begin, although I can say nothing out loud but what I am writing in this letter, you are thinking that I had completely forgotten to write you the promised letter and that I had only remembered upon seeing you and that I had, therefore, sat down next to you and finally began making good on my promise, better late than never, making our meeting a silent and awkward affair as I focused on my writing, seeming not to pay attention to you after so much elapsed time between this and our last meeting, although I am thinking only of you. But that was not the case. I had always intended to write you this letter with you sitting next to me for, truth be told, this letter could not have been written anywhere other than right here, right now, in the past, with me sitting next to you, you waiting for me to finish, nervous as to whether you are in the right to interrupt or whether you should allow me to finish, not realizing that, if you interrupted, you wouldn't really be interrupting anything at all.

                Sincerely,

THE LAST LIGHT YOU'LL SEE

"It's simple, really, when you think about it."

That's what the man behind the counter tells you, over the swirling sound of the wind blowing through the door. It sounds like the ocean.

"When you think about it, really, it's simple," he says, inversely repetitious.

And you can't help but think about it. And you tend to agree. And, you admit, you knew all along. Because you thought about it. Which is the way, or a way, one gets to know things. You were on Route 10, surrounded by cars, surrounded by your car, searching for the place where Routes 10 and 11 merge, where they become one. Your directions told you, still tell you, that to reach your destination, or the point that leads to your ultimate destination, you needed to, you need to continue on 10 until it unites with 11. There was nothing to it. There is nothing to it. Which is the problem. If there were something, no matter what, you could deal with it alone. Instead, you entered the Shell station, an atavism resembling an immense yellow shell, with that feeling. That Lost feeling. Lost in the nothing there was to it. And the problem with that Lost feeling: It isn't easily dispelled. Even when the arguments argue against it. Even when the reasoning reasons against it. Even when the evidence evinces against it. But the feeling was not, is not strong. It is only there. Its foothold is weak. You are confident. Confident in yourself. Confident in your fellow man. Yet, you cannot deny that Lost feeling. Hence, though 10 was (and remains) the correct road, though the map and directions both agreed (and still do) on the inevitable fusion with 11, you had to ask. To double-check. To be safe. To make sure. You left 10, left your car, left the inexpensive petrol, left the bald workman reapplying the letter S to the pumps, left the out-of-doors, and stopped in front of Roy (to give the man behind the counter a name). He's the sort of man you ask directions: flannel shirt, blue jeans, large squarish glasses, black hair, rough hands, leathery skin, amiable smile—if asked to present the prototypical filling-station attendant, you would be hard-pressed to find a better specimen than Roy. He exudes confidence. And placidity. This is a man who has never been lost. Could you travel with him, everywhere, you would know precisely where to go. Always. And that Lost feeling, that anxiety, that twisting of the stomach, gnawing at the brain, that chattering uncertainty, that foul stench of impotence, that paranoia that whispers, "You missed the exit, the directions are wrong, the union of civil engineers has conspired against you, your destination does not exist," would not exist. For Roy would direct you. Roy would say everything's fine.

"Everything's fine," says Roy. "All you need to do is drive back to 10, keep following until you reach the last light you'll see. That's where 10 and 11 meet."

You take one last look at this marvel, an atavism himself, and thank him. Roy. Amongst his clean white tile, clean white walls, clean white shelves, orderly boxes of candy, snacks, bottles of pop, emergency automotive supplies, maps. Inside his yellow shell. Roy.

You are confident you will not have to ask directions again. That all will be smooth sailing.

Outside, you see the hooligans have returned. The pumps are without the letter S once more.

"Let me get that for you," said the girl with the spiky hair. She didn't get up.

Her boyfriend, wearing a blue Mobilgas jumpsuit, chewing gum, stared ahead, sullen.

You opened the door. Another customer (who looked at you strangely) exited. And as you entered, a film display collapsed. A couple of the disposable cameras went off, taking random pictures, firing random flashes that remained before your eyes for seconds afterward as if you were in your own lightning storm. Then you waited. She didn't get up. You stood in the Mobil station off Route 18 with cameras at your feet.

To your knowledge, Roy was right. But before you reached the point where 10 and 11 merge, there was a detour. A bridge was out. The road was being deconstructed. Or reconstructed. There was a terrible accident. Or something. Not for nothing do they close the roads. Not for nothing do they construct signs. A detour. To Route 18. If there's anything worse than that Lost feeling, it's being detoured when you're so close that you can fill in the blank. But your confidence in the world around you, in progression forward, remained firm. A sign lavishly promised, after fifteen miles, that you would reemerge onto 10, that you would find where 10 and 11 become one, that order would be restored to the universe. It was quite a sign. And you trusted the sign. You followed the sign. For signs are to be followed. They lead somewhere. They leave out nothing. Soon it became apparent, however, that 18 was not an oft-traveled road. That you were the sole motorist. That the pavement was alternately rough and smooth, there were more curves than on 10, and it felt as if you'd driven more than fifteen miles, but then what does fifteen miles feel like? Or what *do* fifteen miles feel like? Is there a feeling that marks fifteen miles? At sixty miles per hour, fifteen miles equals fifteen minutes, yet you must *average* sixty miles per hour, and you do not know what your average was, when you think about it (which must also be a way *not* to know things), and you didn't look at the clock when you detoured, and the clock doesn't work, and you didn't look at the odometer, and you found yourself slowing down at intervals, at others driving quite fast, too fast, although you couldn't imagine that the police would patrol an area of, yes, abandoned road this seemingly late at night, whatever time it was. And then: that Lost feeling. And then, you saw the Mobil.

    It's not as clean as the Shell. And there are lights missing. And there's a crazy-looking hairless guy wandering through the pump islands. And it's not well-stocked.

And the gas is more expensive. But it's an acceptable filling station. Anyway, all you need is directions. Are directions. Whatever. And anyone around here should know where 10 and 11 become one. So, amongst the slightly dusty floors, orderly and disorderly shelves, you tell Spiky and Beeman (names, precious names) just where you needed to be. Just where you need to be. Where you need to go. As you reassemble the film display.

"Oh yeah, no problem," says Spiky.

Pause. Gum chewing.

You repeat, in a confident voice, where you need to go.

"Huh," says Spiky. "Where? Oh. To 10/11. Sure."

Beeman, gum-chewer extraordinaire. "You were on 10."

"Why'd you leave?" says Spiky.

"There was a detour."

Beeman stops, removes the gum from his mouth, examines it, returns it to his mouth, recommences.

"Oh," says Spiky.

"Could you help me find 10/11 … again?"

"He knows where it is," says Spiky.

Perhaps he does.

"But we'd need the map," says Spiky.

"Ha–Have you a map?"

"Yeah."

"Oh."

Snap, snap, snap, says Beeman. Or intones Beeman. Or … who cares?

"Let me get it for you," says Spiky. She doesn't move.

Pause.

You ask if she's going to get it.

"Get what?"

"You don't have to be so rude!" screams Beeman. Supposedly. You were looking at Spiky. It could've been someone else. For Beeman is still chewing gum. And appears the same.

"Sorry, he gets like that sometimes. Lemme get the map for you," says Spiky.

Immobile silence in the Mobil station. You can hear the swirling of the wind, the sound of the ocean.

"Make a right out of the drive," says Beeman, looking at a map, procured from somewhere.

"Go down five miles," says Spiky.

"Until …"

"… you reach …"

"… the last light you'll see. …"

"Turn left on 17," says Beeman.

Then the door opens. The film display falls over. Cameras. Flashes. Randomness. Confused rods, cones, retinas. You look at the new customer strangely, hope you won't have to ask directions again, and walk out the door. From behind, you hear gum chewing, and: "Let me get that for you."

At the Pilot station, the fidgety man behind the counter (who is unremarkable save for fidgetiness) does not understand why you're on 17 if you want 10/11. You explain about the detour. Unhelpful. He doesn't comprehend why you ever left 10 if you wanted, if you want, if you'll be wanting 10/11; he is equally in the dark as to why you didn't stay on 10 until you reached 10/11, why you ever took off on a fool's errand like motoring

THE LAST LIGHT YOU'LL SEE

onto 18 and then 17. The word detour is not in his vocabulary. It needs a definition.

detour[1] \dee-too-er\ *noun*

1: A derivation from a direct course; *especially*: a roundabout way temporarily replacing part of a route. **2**: The point where one's route and progression become uncertain due to an unfamiliarity with the course. **3**: A state of duress where one begins to doubt the positive guiding principle of the infrastructure; **3a**: A condition of protracted duress wherein one seriously questions the existence of the infrastructure (and other subsequent structures, complexes, systems, networks), often concluding in a sidebar to a petroleum station, occasionally concluding in confused frustration, rarely ending in a change of address [We were trying to get to Disney World, but because of the *detour* we now live in a section of Montana ... we think.]. **4**: Where one assures himself that everything will be fine; **4a**: Such assurances often begin with the concatenation of route numbers, the necessity of asking directions from unreliable characters such as Spiky and Beeman, who must be familiar with their environs if nothing more, the disarming simplicity of the primary portion of their proposed course (reaching Route 17 from Route 18), until one comes to the realization that returning to Route 18 from Route 17 is impossible because the left lane is unavailable, because of the manifold convolutions at the outset of said route where, often, it appeared as if one were turning onto a different road when, indeed, one continued on Route 17.

detour[2] *intransitive verb*

1: To proceed by a detour. **2**: To move beyond the disarmingly simple and then tortuous portion of one's course, to find oneself on miles of unquestionably straight, profoundly flat land without having one's true course anywhere in sight; **2a:** To drive forward through acres of farmland, farmhouses, bald farmers, barns, bovines; **2b:** To realize that the former plurals were incorrect, that there is but one farmhouse, farmer, barn, bovine repeating, offset only by a mammoth, nacreous shell standing on a platform, lit from below; the shell is inexplicably mocking, as if it comprehends the entirety of the situation and has deduced said situation to be of an amusing nature, filling one with the sensation that should the shell begin chortling, or, to specify, should the creature therein begin guffawing, said creature would issue forth into the universe; **2c:** To question what said creature would be, if there would be signs to indicate its nativity, if there would be lights. **3:** To question how one will know the last light one sees; will one have time to think about it? to know? **4:** To experience that Lost feeling on a continuing basis. **5:** To finally find, adjacent to the farmhouse, a Pilot station with expensive gasoline and chaotic interior.

Fidget still doesn't understand what you're doing at his gas station.

You mention the detour … the road's closed.

"Closed?" he says. "Hell, what a pain in the ass."

You agree.

"Route 10's where you need to be," he says, fidgeting.

You say you want to move on, to go forward, to progress. You want to be confident that no more directions will be needed; you want to, once again, believe in your fellow man. You want to find the point where 10 and 11 become one.

THE LAST LIGHT YOU'LL SEE

Fidget stops fidgeting, so he is now only called "Fidget" as a manner of speaking. He looks at you as if infinitely disappointed. But then he speaks:

"All right, since you can't just go back to 10 via 17 and 18, what you're gonna want to do is take 17 the other way, way down, way far down, until you get to a light, and then you're gonna turn left, no, right, no, it's left, and then you're gonna go for a spell, over some hills, wait, yeah, nope, maybe a couple hills, maybe there ain't, and past a red house with blue shutters and a green door, or maybe a blue house with green shutters and a red door, or maybe a green house with red shutters and a blue door, or maybe, no, wait, they tore that house down, so, oh yeah! they built a new house, bunch of houses, only you can't see 'em from there, and then, after a bit, you're going to bear left, no, right, no, left, but make sure that you don't *turn* right, I mean left, and then you'll be on that road for a while until the last light ... you'll reach? ... you see? ... you'll turn before the light, I mean after you turn right, after the light, I mean, where you'll turn left, I mean right, and then you'll pick up Route 20. Follow 20 for a few miles. You'll see the signs for 10/11. Can't miss it."

detour[3] *transitive verb*

To send by a circuitous route.

On Route 13, in the Janus station, Roy is dressed like Spiky; Beeman is fidgety and confusing and only occasionally chewing gum; Spiky's dressed like Roy; Fidget's dressed in a Mobilgas jumpsuit and chews gum.

Maybe it isn't any of them. Maybe you've lost so much confidence in other people that everyone looks like everyone else. (Sure, keep telling yourself that. If it helps.) There are two shadowy figures in the back. There's a bald guy sitting behind bulletproof glass. He's the clerk. The glass is so dirty that you can hardly see the bald guy. Except, of course, to see that he's bald. He presumably has a microphone to speak into.

A swirling sound comes from the microphone's speaker. It sounds like the ocean. The bald guy says …

… there were red houses with blue shutters and green doors, red houses green shutters blue doors, red houses no shutters green doors, red houses no shutters blue doors, red houses blue shutters no doors, red houses green shutters no doors, blue houses green shutters red doors, blue houses red shutters green doors, blue houses no shutters red doors, blue houses no shutters green doors, blue houses red shutters no doors, blue houses green shutters no doors, green houses red shutters blue doors, green houses blue shutters red doors, green houses no shutters blue doors, green houses no shutters red doors, green houses blue shutters no doors, green houses red shutters no doors, invisible houses with either red or green or blue shutters or doors, invisible houses no shutters red or green or blue doors, invisible houses red or green or blue shutters no doors, invisible houses without any doors or shutters or with invisible doors or shutters always on the horizon, always the house that would signify the coming of Route 20, Route 20 that would take you to your destination, to the point where 10 and 11 become one, but soon you began to believe the houses were figments, that you should attempt to avoid the houses, that you should only drive to those points that opposed what you'd been told up to then, driving straight when you thought you should turn, turning when you thought you should drive straight, turning left when you thought you should turn right, turning right when you thought you should turn left, doubling back when dead ahead grew suspect, driving in reverse for miles and miles just for a change, and since you couldn't trust any of the directions you'd been given anyhow, you tried to lap that LOST feeling by making sure you rebelled against any and all courses, realizing you couldn't trust anyone, no, you couldn't trust anyone but yourself, until you found a Route 13, which you recalled from one of the maps, you recalled it connected to Route 11 somewhere, so you tore down Route 13, paving your own trail (metaphorically speaking), shouting your own directions to yourself, refusing to believe in any of the lies around you, deafening your own ears, challenging that LOST feeling to a duel, realizing you did need gasoline. ...

And then you saw Roy dressed as Spiky. Even with the punked-out hair. Your stomach started to twist. That anxiety, gnawing, chattering, stinking, existing, paranoia.

"... You looking for something?"

"You ... you think you're lost."

"Lost," replies Beeman/Fidget.

"Lost!" says Spiky/Roy, dramatically.

"How can you find your way? How can you ever know where you were in the first place?" existentially questions Fidget. Or Beeman.

"You can't. You just can't," says Roy. Or Spiky.

"You could go to a gas station. Ask directions," says someone or other. It's impossible to tell the characters apart.

"We're practicing for a play," says the bald guy through his poorly amplified, swirly-sounding microphone. "We're the Janus Theater Group. We used to work out of the Last Light Yule. Now we're here."

Pause.

Um. You ask Baldy who he is.

"He's the narrator," someone says. You look to the shadowy characters in the back. They remain backward and deeply enveloped in shadow.

"No, no, no. You're supposed to ask the name of the play," says Baldy.

"What is the … uh? Narrator? A play?" you say, rhymingly.

"A play?"

"A play!"

"I thought you'd never ask."

"What kind of play?"

"What's that you say?"

"A play, a play, a play."

"There's going to be a play."

"There will be singing."

"There will be dancing."

"There will be singing and dancing."

"Dancing and singing together!"

"Sdianngciinngg!"

The shadowy characters emerge wearing a Chinese dragon costume, swinging sinuously about, the players sing and dance but to their own individual songs and dances performed simultaneously, although the one uniform movement is a whirlpool of prancing playactors, and the dragon loves it, the dancing amidst the chaos, he loves it, and any minute you expect airborne candy bars, bottles of pop to smash into the ground erupting, potato chips, peanuts, pretzels, crackers to fly into the air, windshield washer fluid oil antifreeze transmission fluid cascading to the tile and leaking everywhere, magazines, lighters, cigarettes, cigars, playing cards, water, beer, wine, ice scrapers, novelty items to explode off the shelves, until you see there are no shelves to support any of those products, there are no products, you had only assumed them because gas stations ... certainly sell ... no ... and all the items you thought were in the station are replaced by whiteness, a whiteness not like Roy's, but a nacreous white, and you're in a large, nacreous room without doors or windows or anything save a booth where the narrator sits behind bulletproof glass, save players cavorting around a Chinese dragon that revels amongst them all.

"I just wanted to find my way," you say, once more rhyming.

"Suppose you ask directions," says the narrator.

"Why?"

"Because you look like the kind of person who asks directions. Plus, it's in the script."

"Oh. Then: can you give me some directions?"

"I don't know. Where you going?"

Pause.

"Route 10/11."

"That's easy! Route 13's the only road that can take you to the road that'll get you to 10/11. So, take 13 to Route 6 which connects directly with 10/11. So, what you're gonna do is, you're gonna go back out, get in your car, take 13 to 6, keep going on 6 until you reach the Last Light Yule. ..."

"The last light you'll?"

"Sí ... from there, you'll make a right onto 10/11."

"But … this LOST … how will I … how will it all end?"

Remaining hazy behind the bulletproof glass, the narrator says, swirlingly: "That's easy! It'll end like this:"

The Cave Station, located on an unknown route, is built into the side of a lone, bleak mountain. Upon entering, a man who is either sleeping or dead (undead?) steps behind you, blocking the exit. Another man sits behind a counter looking at you, nonplussed. Give them some names if you'd like. If it will calm your nerves. If it will instill a shred of confidence. Of false hope. Behind the man behind the counter is the gaping maw of a cave, pitch black. From the cave you hear a swirling sound. It sounds like the ocean. Otherwise, there is nothing. There is always nothing, if nothing else.

The worst thing is. Is the idea you'll. You'll never find your way again. And the longer you remain. The longer it lasts. The feeling amplifies. To such an extent that. It includes all else. Metaphysically trapped. Unable to advance. Advance toward your goal. Ceasing to progress. Ceasing to move forward. You move into the neighborhood. If one surrounds you. Or into the country. If that's what it is. The Great Wide Open. There. You would never find your way. You would never. Never be able to return. It's as if. As if you've slipped. Slipped into a foreign dimension. Where your destinations. Don't exist. And your old purlieus. Never did. Route 6, a resemblance. No matter. The distance covered. Couldn't imagine. Reaching your. Thought perhaps. Perhaps you weren't driving. Perhaps the road was moving. An asphalt whirlpool. Directing you. Nowhere special. Giving you. No signs. Nothing. To think about. Nothing. To know. Nothing.

"You need help," says the man in front of the yawning abyss. It could be a question or a statement.

"I ... I was ... I was on Route 6."

"No Route 6 anywhere around here," says Whatshisname.

"I'm ... I'm trying ... to get to Route 10/11."

"No such thing."

"I'm ... I'm trying ... to find the place ... where 10 and 11 become ... one."

"Routes 10 and 11 never meet. And they certainly never become Route 1."

"But ... I was told ... I was told they ... What?"

"Where you going?"

"I'm ... I'm ... uh ..."

"Well, you can't leave that way. You have to go this way."

"But it's a cave."

"It is. Go down through the cave. Keep going until you reach the last light."

"The last light? How will I know?"

"You'll see."

You shuffle through the cave, surrounded by the swirling sound. It is dark. There are no lights. You cannot see ahead or behind you. Until you feel yourself being directed. When the person speaks, you know him to be the narrator; you know him to be me. I say:

The darkness of the cave, growing thicker each league, now melts away and is replaced by the semi-darkness of a starry night. You are driving. Pretend it's Route 6, or 10/11, or 1, if you wish. Yet it is none of these. In the distance you see a large, nacreous shell that is closed. Up above there is Ursa Major, whirlpool galaxies, and Draco. But soon the serene, starry sky is covered by storm clouds issuing forth from the shell. The storm is a driving storm: there is thunder, there is lightning. The dancing characters from before surround you; a few are identifiable, legions are shadowy. And then you see that the road is a whirlpool of asphalt, you are not driving, you are barely able to keep your automobile on the road, and this hydroplaning and turning about is your slidestep and pirouette, your dance. Soon, the dragon joins you, climbing out of the shell, cavorting, reveling amongst the shadowy and identifiable. The lightning grows more intense; the thunder rumbles louder. The dragon loves the storm, loves the confusion of characters, of people you will never know, loves the thunder, loves the rain, loves the lightning, loves that *Lost* feeling that is now so puissant, so persistent you would be lost without it; yet you wonder how this could've happened—you only meant to progress toward your destination by automobile. What could be more prosaic? How could it end in this? You wonder if the next swirling street will be yours, will deliver you to, the point where … And the lightning gets closer, the dragon a silhouette, your eyes unable to adjust, staring as if you were staring into the flash of a camera, and the characters dance, the shell explodes, the thunder grows louder still, the lightning closer, closer, until the white from the electrical storm fills your field of vision, but still you are not sure if this is the last light you'll see. It's not something you know. You'll have to think about it.

ABOUT THE AUTHOR

Andrew Farkas is the author of *The Great Indoorsman: Essays*, *The Big Red Herring*, *Sunsphere*, and *Self-Titled Debut*. He is associate professor of creative writing at Washburn University and an editor for *Always Crashing*. You can find him at thegreatindoorsman.org.

ACKNOWLEDGMENTS

"Timbuktu" was previously published in *Emprise Review* #4.

"Delusions of Nandeur" was previously published in *Whiskey Island Magazine* #53.

"Bastille Day" was previously published in *Sidebrow* #1 and *White Horse*.

"An Immaterial Message" was previously published in *The Brooklyn Rail* (January 2005/December 2006).

"The Divine Plan: Notes for an Unperformable Mise-en-Scène" was previously published in *The Brooklyn Rail* (May 2007).

"A Sky Party" was previously published in *The Cincinnati Review* #6.1.

"Astray" was previously published in *The Brooklyn Rail* (June 2010).

"Identity Theft" was previously published in *The Brooklyn Rail* (June 2009).

"Oubliette" was previously published in *BlazeVox* (2007).

"The First Circumnavigator" was previously published in *Pank* #5.

"A Rogue Department Course Offering" was previously published in *The Brooklyn Rail* (December 2013).

"Is This the Ship of Theseus?" was previously published in *Western Humanities Review* #68.2.

"Written with You Sitting Next to Me" was previously published in *Another Chicago Magazine* #50.2.

AUTHOR THANKS

I would especially like to thank Donald Breckenridge, the former fiction editor of *The Brooklyn Rail*, for regularly publishing my work from 2005-2013. I recall walking into Mildew Hall at the University of Alabama and having Michael Martone excitedly tell me that I needed to contact Donald. It turns out that Donald liked an overly long piece I submitted but couldn't publish it because of the length. If I'd start writing shorter pieces, though, he'd publish them frequently. And so, he did.

Big thanks also go to Leah Angstman for reviving this book. I'm so glad to be joining the Alternating Current Press line crew!

I was extremely lucky to have had Elisabeth Sheffield as my first editor. Thank you for all of your help and for ushering me into the world of book publishing!

Thank you also to all of my awesome blurbers: Jesi Bender, Gabriel Blackwell, Brian Evenson, Lily Hoàng, Michael Martone, Aimee Parkison, and Hugh Sheehy.

Finally, this book is dedicated to the memories of Clyde Jentoft and Allen Wier. R.I.P.

Professor Jentoft was my teacher when I was an undergrad at Kent State University. He looked like the bust of Socrates, and we called him Socrates behind his back. He said that if he were to believe in a deity, that deity would be William Shakespeare. At the time, I said if I believed in a deity, it'd be Kurt Vonnegut. As Vonnegut, the secular humanist, might jokingly say: Professor Jentoft is in heaven now.

Allen Wier was my professor at the University of Tennessee. After one class, I asked Allen if he was headed to the bar. Our seminar sometimes went out, sometimes didn't. I was new to Knoxville and hadn't really made any friends yet. Allen asked, "Who's all going?" I said that if he and I were going, then there'd be two people at least. We went to the bar. The last time I saw him was in Minneapolis at AWP 2015. I told him about this memory. He remembered.

COLOPHON

The edition you are holding is the First Edition of this publication in this form and contains the reprinted pieces from the out-of-print *Self-Titled Debut*, along with new material.

The title font and drop caps are set in AlterEgo, created by I Do Not Sleep. The secondary title font is set in Amperzand, created by A. J. Paglia. The Alternating Current Press logo is set in Portmanteau, created by JLH Fonts. Headers and footers are set in Avenir Book, created by Adrian Frutiger in collaboration with Monotype Type director Akira Kobayashi. All other text is set in Iowan Old Style, created by John Downer. All fonts used with permission and full commercial license; all rights reserved.

Cover jacket designed by Leah Angstman, with artwork by Patter Hill. The Alternating Current lightbulb logo was created by Leah Angstman, © 2013, 2026 Alternating Current Press. The devil section divider was created by Hades Minion 13, courtesy of Clker. Some artwork is governed under a Pixabay Content License. Author photo by Nick Krug. All images used with permission and full commercial license; all rights reserved.

Other Works from
ALTERNATING CURRENT PRESS

All of these books (and more) are available at
Alternating Current's website: altcurrentpress.com.

altcurrentpress.com

Made in the USA
Coppell, TX
22 February 2026

72098656R00121